Thumbprint Mysteries

W9-ALM-533

# THE HIDDEN MEN

## BY

## STEPHEN F. WILCOX

CONTEMPORARY BOOKS

*a division of* NTC/CONTEMPORARY PUBLISHING GROUP
Lincolnwood, Illinois USA

YA
WIL

Thumbprint
Mysteries

# MORE THUMBPRINT MYSTERIES

by Stephen F. Wilcox:

*The Hard Time Cafe*
*Purgatory Prayers*

This is a work of fiction. The characters, incidents, and dialogues are products of the author's imagination and are not to be construed as real. Any resemblance to actual events or persons, living or dead, is entirely coincidental.

Cover Illustration: Adam Niklewicz

ISBN: 0-8092-0605-6

Published by Contemporary Books,
a division of NTC/Contemporary Publishing Group, Inc.,
4255 West Touhy Avenue,
Lincolnwood (Chicago), Illinois 60646-1975 U.S.A.
© 1999 Stephen F. Wilcox
Manufactured in the United States of America.

9 0 QB 0 9 8 7 6 5 4 3 2 1

# CHAPTER 1

Brother Malthius, coming out of morning mass at 6:15, ducked his head to hide a yawn. He had been up since two and active since breakfast at three A.M., but it wouldn't do for the others to see his weariness. They'd been up just as long as he, after all.

*You'd think you'd be used to it by now,* he chided himself, as he left the chapel by the side door. For fifteen years he'd been rising in the dead of night and spending a half hour praying on his knees beside the cot in his cell. He'd have a breakfast of coffee, dry raisin bread, and watery fruit juice. Then two hours of labor, usually in the bakery, loading flour and other raw ingredients into the giant mixers, before lauds and morning Mass commenced at 5:30.

A typical beginning, then, and no excuse for his sloth. Brother Malthius, after all, was only thirty-seven, a mere

1

babe at an abbey where the average age was past fifty. But he was a weak man, physically and morally; he recognized this in himself and prayed constantly to become worthy of this monastery and of his brethren and, most of all, worthy in the eyes of God.

Still, he couldn't always overcome his weaknesses, and the worst of them was this chronic fatigue. He retired to his cell each night at 7:30, as did the others. But unlike them, he had difficulty falling asleep after evening devotions. Winters weren't so bad with the early darkness, but the summer months, such as now, with a high sun and the warmth of his tiny cell, were problematic.

The thing was, no matter how hard he toiled during the day, working in the bakery or the fields or the laundry, his mind was never as tired as his body. He'd lie on his cot in his ten-by-ten cell, and his brain would run wild, dozens of random thoughts colliding. It could be anything, on any subject. The moment of the creation of the universe, examined in both theological and cosmological terms. The vaguely recalled taste of a hot fudge sundae or a barefoot stroll through the wet grass of a city park. A childhood memory of family outings or family disputes.

Anything.

He'd been called to the insular world of the Trappist monks as a very young man—a boy, really. It had seemed a literal godsend to him, this confused teenager from a broken home. The abbey offered tranquillity in place of chaos, security in place of fear, commitment in place of loss and abandonment.

He had come close to joining the army instead, but he was afraid he wouldn't get past the physical demands of basic training and he was repulsed by violence. He had thought about the priesthood too, but the priesthood was a call to serve other sinners like himself, and he knew he did not have that calling. He was much too introverted to minister to the poor and the wretched, blessed though they be.

Which left the Trappists and the Abbey of the Ganannoqua. To Brother Malthius, the chance to serve God directly, through his daily prayers and his modest labors, had seemed the perfect solution.

But that was fifteen long years ago. It somehow had not dawned on him, in those apprentice years, that the abbey was a world of morning men and that he, alas, was a night person.

He had talked it over with the abbot, Father Mazewski, on several occasions, this weakness of his. The abbot was a much more worldly man than Brother Malthius. A Korean War veteran and a lawyer, he had joined the priesthood and then the Trappist order after his young wife had died of cancer some thirty years ago. It helped that Father Mazewski thought Brother Malthius was being too hard on himself and counseled that he try reading himself to sleep on these long summer evenings.

"A glass of warm milk and some Teilhard de Chardin," the abbot had suggested with a twinkle, or perhaps Thomas Merton or Thomas Aquinas would do.

And the advice had helped, particularly the part about reading de Chardin. A few pages, a few paragraphs even, and Brother Malthius's eyelids began to droop.

But then there were the dreams to contend with. Crazy kaleidoscope dreams. Sometimes—and he hesitated to admit this, even to himself—vivid, mortifying dreams, about this or that comely young woman he might chance to see at the visitor's center or the gift shop.

"Oh, Lord, save me from myself," he muttered

fervently as he descended the garden path, moving with assurance despite the weak light of early morning.

It was his practice to detour down to the grotto after morning Mass for a few moments of fresh air and solitude. Solitude without the expectation of prayer, that is. Some quiet time to relax, unobserved, and enjoy the natural world in peace and quiet. Some mornings he'd spot a raccoon returning to its tree after a night's forage, or perhaps a family of red foxes slipping in and out amongst the Stations of the Cross on the way back to their underground lair just east of the grotto's woods, out past the pond.

Brother Malthius found his favorite spot, a stone bench near the depiction of Christ ascending Calvary, and seated himself, smoothing the folds of his habit. He let his eyes drift across the deeply shadowed woods and paths, over the fourteen familiar life-sized wood carvings of Christ's labor with the cross. Looking at nothing in particular but hoping to spy some movement that would betray the presence of wildlife.

He said later that he must have seen the crumpled form near Christ ascending Calvary immediately upon arriving at his bench, but that it took several moments before his brain registered that it was there. Something out of place in the familiar landscape. A low, lumpy mass—like a pile of freshly dug soil—lying to the side of the path, obscured by the gray morning light of the woods.

Brother Malthius would not call himself a man of great insight. But on that one occasion, as he moved with fear from his bench toward the still form, he somehow knew that he would never again find tranquillity in the wooded grotto of the Abbey of the Ganannoqua.

*    *    *

"Br-Br-Brother J-J-John!"

Brother Malthius burst into the bakery, seizing upon the first person he came to, who was Brother Gabriel, the head baker.

"Shush," Brother Gabriel cautioned him, his index finger held rigid against his lips. Noisy outbursts were not tolerated at the abbey. Although there was no absolute requirement in the Trappist order, several of the monks had taken vows of silence and those who hadn't nevertheless kept spoken communication to a minimum. Sign language was customary, but sometimes insufficient, as was the case now, given Brother Malthius's high state of excitement.

*Brother John is not here*, Brother Gabriel signed rapidly. *He's probably in the office at this hour, fussing over that computer—*

"No!" Brother Malthius's shout drowned out the thrum of the three big stainless steel mixers. "He's not in the office! He's not anywhere! He's—oh, dear Lord!"

"Calm yourself, Mal." Brother Gabriel's voice came out thick from lack of use. Other monks began to leave their work and gather around as he gripped the younger monk by the shoulders. "What's happened? Has John fallen ill—?"

"He's fallen—he's fallen—" Brother Malthius's mouth dropped open, the cheeks of his thin sunburned face formed hollows, and he groaned loudly. To Brother Gabriel, who had once lectured on fine arts before coming to the monastic life, he resembled Edvard Munch's famous painting, *The Scream*.

Then, as surely as the panic arose, it subsided. Brother Malthius's brown eyes blinked once, slowly. The emotion, as well as the color, drained from his face and he said quietly, "Brother John has been murdered."

*     *     *

"Looks like a knife wound."

Sergeant Podesta, a sheriff's investigator for Lorret County, was on one knee next to the body. The late Brother John lay on his side now, having been turned to that position by Podesta as soon as the crime scene photographer had finished shooting the body and the surrounding area. The front of the coarse brown robe he was wearing was pulled up, revealing a pair of gray workman's pants and thick-soled work shoes beneath; revealing, too, a thin, bloody puncture wound six inches below the left armpit.

"That's what it is all right, Sarge," said one of the medical technicians standing by. "Some kind of thin, sharp blade anyway, long enough to nick the heart."

"Get somebody combing these woods hereabouts for the murder weapon," Podesta instructed the deputy assigned to assist him. "Whoever did the deed may've chucked it someplace. Happens a lot, a crime like this."

The deputy, whose name was Trabold, wanted to ask what the sergeant meant by "a crime like this," but he didn't for fear of showing his ignorance. Instead, he suggested, "Maybe the perp threw it in the pond out there. That's about the best place to get rid of it, like permanently."

Podesta looked at him. "Whatever. Right now get somebody searching these woods. We'll worry about dragging the pond later if we have to."

With the deputy gone, Podesta resumed watching the technicians carefully work the area around the body. Brother John Kolumus, in life, had been hardy—nearly six feet tall, over two hundred pounds, and quite fit for a man past sixty. An outdoors type, no doubt, equally at home chopping wood and swinging a hoe in the abbey's vast gardens as singing in the chapel or kneeling reverently before one of these woodland statuaries. Now, as he lay there in his hooded robe, the bloody puncture in the side of his rib cage, he looked the way all murder victims looked to Sergeant Podesta—like a threat to his retirement plans.

Lorret County had had five homicides in the past year, four of which were domestic in nature—husbands killing wives mostly, with one instance of a woman committing infanticide. In each of those cases, the perpetrator was obvious from the get-go—a drunken man standing over the body holding a shotgun or a carving knife and crying how he didn't mean to do it, that sort of thing.

The fifth case was unsolved and was likely to stay that way. The remains of a young female had been found out in a field earlier that spring, buried in a grave so shallow that a farmer's plow had uncovered it on the first pass. The body had been in the ground at least six months, according to the coroner's office, and was badly decomposed. Apparently a strangulation victim, late teens or early twenties, probably a runaway or a prostitute from Riverton. But no identification had been made yet and Podesta doubted there ever would be. If a girl like that had any family, they had probably long since given up on her—lost her to drugs and the street. The sad truth was if friends and relatives didn't care, nobody else would, either, and the case would remain on the books but forgotten.

*No such luck with the murder of this monk,* Podesta thought gloomily. *Especially not in an election year.* The sheriff wouldn't even wait for the serious media to descend from up in Riverton; he'd be on Podesta's ass to nail the perp before the ink dried on the morning paper.

He sighed and glanced around. Everything appeared normal within the forty-foot perimeter of the yellow crime-scene tape. Forensics technicians were scouring the ground for anything out of place, including a weapon; the medical techs were readying the body for the medical examiner. His trainee, Deputy Trabold, was organizing a couple of the other uniforms to search the rest of the woods.

It was only when Podesta widened his viewpoint that things began to look hinky. Fifty feet away, near one of the life-sized carvings, the one showing somebody— Podesta wasn't religious—helping Jesus pick up the cross, were gathered half a dozen monks. They were staring, mostly at him, those deep-set eyes and thin faces and heads of closely cropped hair reminding him of old black-and-white photos of concentration camp victims.

Like a guilty conscience following him around. And with clout too. Maybe they weren't political themselves, but these Trappists ran the biggest bakery in the county right here on the grounds of the abbey. And while they did the bulk of the work themselves, they still used locals to help out with the baking, to make deliveries, to buy supplies. All of which translated into jobs, and jobs translated into money, and money always—always—drew in the politicians. And nowhere on the planet were there politicians more partisan, more voter-sensitive, more beholden to special interests than in a small county sheriff's department.

Sergeant Podesta looked up at the life-sized carving of Christ lugging that big heavy cross uphill to his doom and he thought, *Jesus, you and me both.*

# CHAPTER 2

"To be a monk, Sergeant, means to live the gospel in an extreme way. We seek the face of God in our daily lives, every day, through humility, simplicity of living, obedience to Christ, respect for one another. These are some of the rules handed down by Benedict fifteen centuries ago." The abbot was a tall, slim, bespectacled man, who looked to be about fifty but was actually well past sixty. His voice was calm, soothing, like the classical music that played faintly in the background. But there was something else behind the words and behind those prescription lenses: gray steel eyes that didn't flinch.

"Let me reverse roles for a moment, Sergeant, and ask you a question. What would you think would be the most difficult aspect of monastic life? The hardest thing to get used to, if you will."

Sergeant Podesta almost blurted out "No sex" but

caught himself in time. He doubted that's what the abbot was going for and, besides, Podesta had been married for twenty-two years to a woman who still undressed with the lights off. He knew that getting along without sex wasn't that tough once you got used to it.

"Uh, maybe the food?" he ventured, knowing this, too, would be wrong, but at least it wouldn't ruffle any feathers.

The abbot allowed himself a small smile. "Well, it's true we'll never win any culinary awards. That is part of the simplicity we strive for. Simple, honest food we raise ourselves, no meat, no special sauces or condiments. No butter, even, for the bread that sustains us at every meal." He leaned forward, and Podesta could feel a tangent coming on. "That's a story in itself, Sergeant. Because we use no butter on our bread, one of the brothers, years ago now, came up with a recipe that added more flavor and body to the bread itself. Well, as you know, once the outside world got a taste of it, an enterprise was born. Thirty years later we're producing nearly fifty thousand loaves of Thy Daily Bread a week for public consumption."

"Yeah, that's interesting, Father, but, uh—"

"Mmm. I've gotten off the point, haven't I? No, Sergeant, the food isn't the most difficult part of being a monk. It's the sameness. Getting used to every day being like the previous day and like all the days to come after, with no breaks, no weekends off, no trips to the movies, no holidays to look forward to. And not just getting used to it, but embracing that sameness as a welcome thing, because it's what helps us get closer to God."

Father Mazewski could see the meaning behind the words was lost on the other man. "Look, Sergeant, my point is this: the monastery is a place where the entire focus is on making ourselves open and available to

Christ. To do this, we strip ourselves of as much of the world as we can. We become hidden men, if you will, hidden away from the bustle of everyday life outside the abbey. Not because we dislike or fear or feel superior to our fellow man, but because we desire to become closer to God. And anything that helps us to achieve that goal, we embrace as a necessary tool of our mission.

"I tell you all this so that you might understand that silence, when we choose to invoke it, is not a retreat from the world. It's simply a further effort to make ourselves available to Christ. A welcome mat laid out to the Word of God. He who would hear must listen!"

Podesta worked his gum a moment longer, invoking his own silence. Now he understood where the abbot was headed with the theology lesson, and he didn't like the direction.

"Yeah, well, listen, uh, Father Mazewski," he said, the anger in his voice barely controlled. "I don't care if this hermit monk of yours has taken a vow of silence or not. He lives in that cave down there and he maybe saw or heard something and I need to question him."

"I understand what you're saying, Sergeant. There's no need to raise your voice. We're all quite distraught as it is, what with the death of Brother John—"

"The *murder* of Brother John. Which is why I need to interview everyone, especially a guy who lives in a cave not fifty yards from where the body was found."

"It isn't actually a cave, Sergeant. It's an old root cellar, dug into the side of the hill years ago, before we had permanent buildings with basements here at the abbey."

"Whatever." Podesta's sigh fluttered the curtains. "Look, I just need to talk to the old fellow, that's all."

"And I've tried to explain why that isn't possible.

Brother Jerome hasn't spoken a word in half a century—"

"Don't you people care that one of your own has been murdered?!"

"Of course we care!" For the first time, the abbot's voice lost its cool precision. "Look around you, man. The men are numb with grief, listless and lost. I hope I can rally them at sext—our midday prayer—by reminding them that Brother John has achieved what we all wish for ourselves ultimately. He's now at the feet of Christ. It's essential at a time like this that we remember who we are and why we're here, Sergeant Podesta. I can't— I *won't* allow your investigation to intrude any more than is absolutely necessary."

Silence fell between the men like a temporary truce at a battle whose outcome was still in doubt. The abbot leaned back, regaining his calm, and studied Podesta, while the policeman let his eyes inventory the room. They were in the abbot's small study, a spare, white-walled space with a plain desk, a desk chair, and a straight-back chair for guests. The best feature of the room was the double window, which looked out to the east toward the vegetable gardens. Several of the monks, dressed in dark green work clothes and straw hats, were out there now, bent and toiling under the late-morning sun. It would've looked like something out of a medieval tapestry, except for one thing.

"They're not wearing robes," Podesta observed absently. "The victim was wearing a sort of robe, but nothing like your outfit. It was more a brown hooded thingy over a pair of work pants."

"Out in the fields, we find trousers and shirts more practical for the work. The 'thingy,' as you put it, we call a smock, which is comfortable in most conditions and for most tasks, but not all. What I'm wearing, the white robe and black scapular, is our formal habit." Father Mazewski steepled his fingers on the desktop. "Now, as for interviewing Brother Jerome, may I suggest you submit a written list of questions and have him write out his responses?"

The sheriff's investigator was shaking his head. "How'm I supposed to get a read on the guy from a list of questions? I need to talk to him myself, look into his eyes when he responds to my—"

"Sergeant, you're talking as if Brother Jerome were a suspect." The abbot was clearly dumbfounded at the idea. "You've seen him. He's eighty-nine years old. He's hard of hearing; his night vision is almost nonexistent. I doubt he'd have the strength to strike someone down with a knife or any other weapon, let alone the inclination."

"Well—still. It ain't by the book."

"We're guided by a different book here, Sergeant," the abbot said. "Anyway, you take written depositions all the time for court purposes, I'm sure. You'll just have to do the same thing in this instance."

Podesta decided that arguing any further with a local religious leader—one who oversaw an expensive bakery operation, to boot—was not an smart move. But he wasn't ready to surrender his argument meekly.

"You said something earlier about how you all pray together like several times a day, beginning first thing in the morning. Is that right?"

"Yes." Father Mazewski drew out the word. "Seven times daily, we come together to sing the psalms in praise of Christ, in addition to morning and evening Mass. There's vigils at 3:30 in the morning, lauds at 5:30, terce at 8:15, sext at noon, none—" Pronounced *no-nay*. "—at 1:00, vespers at 6:00, and compline at 7:30. After which we retire to our cells and begin what we call the grand silence," he added pointedly, "which ends the next morning at vigils."

"So how come nobody noticed the vic—Brother John was missing this morning?" Podesta thumbed open his notepad. "Your Brother Malthius came across the body around 6:20 this morning. The techs at the scene say he'd most likely been dead at least an hour, maybe two. That means Brother John missed the 5:30 prayer thing, lauds, and maybe the earliest one too. Vigils?"

"Yes. At three-thirty. But he didn't miss vigils. I can vouch for that myself, since I spoke with him briefly afterward."

Podesta's head came up from his pad. "What was that about?"

"Our conversation? Nothing significant. I merely took him aside to one of our conversing rooms—"

"Conversing rooms?"

"There are several on the complex. We designate them for use whenever sign language is insufficient. In this case, I wanted to speak to John about his request to go to a full bake on Thursdays." Seeing Podesta's confusion, the abbot explained, "We bake bread three mornings a week, Sergeant, Wednesday, Thursday, and Saturday. Wednesday and Saturday we're at full capacity, about twenty thousand loaves each day, but on Thursday we traditionally do a half-bake, about ten thousand loaves."

"Okay," Podesta nodded. "And Brother John wanted to increase production for some reason."

"Yes, to help meet demand in a new market he was hoping to develop downstate. Brother John is—was—our business manager for bakery operations. He asked me to assess the mood of the other monks regarding increasing our output, and I was reporting some of my findings this morning."

"Which were?"

The abbot shrugged his white-robed shoulders. "Not that it has any relevance, but some of the men are opposed to the idea."

"Why's that? I'd figure anything that brought in more money would be seen as a good thing."

"Well, Sergeant, you have to understand the philosophy that undergirds a Christian monastery. We're all founded on Benedictine principles, which, among other things, require that a monastery support itself through its own useful labors, meaning we must produce a product that can be sold. Yet the rule of Benedict also stipulates that we make a product with integrity, that we sell it at a fair price, and that we produce *only what's needed to do God's work and no more.*"

"Ah. And some of the brothers think you're already making enough bread to live on, is that it?"

"Basically, yes. Of course, what constitutes God's work is subject to interpretation. Brother John was one of those who believed we could send more profits overseas to fund projects in Latin America and Africa and elsewhere. Others feel that if we spend too much time thinking about making bread—and money—we lose sight of our singular objective here at the abbey, which is to be monks. Prayer and contemplation must always be first and foremost."

"I see." A classic case of liberals versus conservatives; just like politics. Podesta scribbled a note in his pad. "Maybe you should give me the names of some of these monks, the ones who didn't like Brother John's expansion plans."

Once again, the abbot's jaw dropped. "You're not suggesting that one of the brothers killed John! That's ridiculous, Sergeant. Utterly unfathomable."

"Why? They're not all as old and feeble as Brother Jerome, are they?"

"Of course not, but this is a religious order! We do not go around murdering each other!"

The sheriff's investigator slapped the notepad shut and exhaled heavily. "Well, somebody killed Brother John Kolumus with a knife on these grounds not more than six hours ago. Now, if none of the men who live here did the deed, then who in the hell did?"

"I'm sure I have no idea," the abbot said. "People, laypeople, come and go every day from this abbey—"

"At four o'clock in the morning?"

"Not normally, no. But it could happen. Anyone familiar with the grounds could virtually come and go as they please in the dark hours, unnoticed. But I can't think of a single person who—"

He stopped so abruptly the last word still formed an O on his lips. The steel-gray eyes seemed to lose focus for a split second behind their glass shields, time enough for Podesta to notice and respond.

"What?" He leaned forward in the stiff-back chair. "You've thought of somebody."

"Well, there is a young man—a boy, really, who's been assisting Brother John." The abbot stared down at his fingers as they nervously drummed the desktop. "A talented, but troubled, young man."

# CHAPTER
# 3

Fifty miles north of the Abbey of the Ganannoqua was the city of Riverton. On the east side of the city, on a busy urban street called Carson Avenue, was Corpus Christi Catholic Church. The pastor of Corpus Christi, a bearded, red-haired man in his early forties, was Father Joe Costello.

That Thursday afternoon at around one-thirty, Father Joe was in his large, Victorian office on the second floor of the rectory. He was listening with increasing gravity to a phone call he'd just received from Father Mazewski.

"Dear Lord. Not Brother John. Why would anyone want to harm—? . . ." His soft blue eyes widened as shock moved over to make room for alarm. "Sean Carpenter! No! It can't be. What makes them suspect—? . . . Yes, I see, but that doesn't mean he had anything to do— . . . Gone? He's—? . . . Oh, my dear Lord."

When the conversation ended, Father Joe replaced the

phone. After a moment, he shook off his despair and made the sign of the cross before saying a silent prayer for Brother John. And a second prayer for young Sean Carpenter.

Five minutes later he was standing at the window, gazing out at the bustling street scene below, when Sister Matthew knocked and entered. He'd forgotten completely about their meeting to discuss an upcoming trip to Arcadia State Penitentiary, to attend a parole review hearing for one of the inmates there. She was her usual self, cheerful and bustling, small but sturdy, dressed in loose khaki slacks and a dark green, oversized, short-sleeved shirt. Formality was not the rule at Corpus Christi, as confirmed by Father Joe's worn jeans and Youth Outreach Program softball team T-shirt.

"A Mr. Sewell, first name Rundell," she reminded him, wagging a thin file folder in the air as she crossed the room. "He's done seven years on an assortment of burglary charges, his second time inside. He's been taking remedial courses for five years now, and he's undertaken the prison's vocational and drug rehab programs as well."

She went on, proposing the man as a good candidate for Corpus Christi's parolee program, but Father Joe wasn't listening.

"Sister, please." The priest shook his head, then collapsed back into his desk chair. "I'm sorry, I just can't concentrate on these matters now. I—I've just received some terrible news. Just—terrible."

"Gracious." The little nun quickly put aside the file and took the chair next to the desk. Wrinkles of concern etched her forehead. "What's happened, Father?"

"You remember Sean Carpenter?"

"Of course." Who could forget Sean? Even among the dozens of troubled kids that had come through the church's Youth Outreach Program in Matty's years at Corpus Christi, Sean Carpenter stood out. Not because his life was any more violent or sadder than the others, but because Sean was exceptionally gifted.

It had been three summers ago, at fifteen, that the boy had first entered the program on an "or else" referral from a family court judge. The "or else" part meant either the boy could join Father Joe's program and show progress over a period of two years, or he could go directly to the state's Industrial Arts School for Boys for those same two years. Industry, as it was known, was a rural reform school for youthful offenders. Delinquent boys from all over the state were housed in dormitories on an old C.C.C. campus that was surrounded by a twelve-foot fence topped with razor wire and guarded by unarmed but well-trained "security personnel."

Little wonder that, given the choice, Sean Carpenter opted for Corpus Christi's homier approach to character building.

Like most of the boys, Sean came into the program expecting to scam his way through the two years. Growing up in a deteriorating housing project with a drug-addicted mother and an abusive father, who came around about as often as a census taker, had taught the boy survival tactics and little else. His only family, as far as he was concerned, was the Backus Avenue Boys. The Back Boys, as they were also known, were a tight-knit gang of teenage boys who thought they ran the streets around Backus Avenue on Riverton's north side. In truth, they were pawns caught between the drug pushers who ran the crack-and-smack houses in the neighborhood and the cops who tried to shut them down.

The Back Boys used the youngest members to do most of the dirty work—drug deliveries, house burglaries, armed robbery at the few ATM machines still operating within a two-mile radius of the neighborhood. The older gang members—those who had reached their seventeenth birthdays and were thus eligible to be tried as adults—limited their own activities to ordering around the young ones and providing muscle whenever anyone came into the 'hood needing "attitude adjustment." This included members of other gangs looking to extend their turf, or a desperate parent trying to rescue his son from falling in with the Back Boys, or even some social welfare do-gooder who strayed too far off the Avenue.

Sean Carpenter's specialty for the Back Boys was burglary. At fifteen, when he entered the Corpus Christi program, he had already been arrested twice for breaking and entering modest homes on the north side. He'd also had previous brushes with the law for shoplifting and truancy. The boy was considered borderline by the judge handling his case. Father Joe's Youth Outreach Program was to be his absolute last chance. Any foul-ups would send him swiftly to Industry, which for many of the boys was a dress rehearsal for Arcadia, the maximum-security prison upstate.

None of this seemed to worry Sean, however, in those early days at Corpus Christi. Father Joe and Sister Matty both remembered well the boy's bad attitude, the cock-sure air of a kid who thinks he's seen it all, done it all. The usual approaches didn't seem to help—placement in a foster home near the church, direct daily counseling from Father Joe himself, tutoring. Sean answered every attempt to bring him in, to make him a part of life at Corpus Christi, with a sneer and a snarl. Then two things happened to turn things around.

The first came in the form of a tall, lanky ex-biker named William Lee Ralston, or Billboard to his friends, so named for the numerous tattoos that adorned his arms and chest. Currently, Billboard was the head chef at The Hard

Time Cafe, a restaurant operated by ex-cons, another of Father Joe's outreach efforts. In his old life, Billboard was a biker and brawler, a kid who had graduated from smoking grass and joyriding in other people's cars to doing smack and doing time. That experience made him the perfect mentor for Sean Carpenter.

The parolees called it "Hell Night." Once a week for two hours or more, half a dozen of the parolees gathered after-hours in the dining room of the restaurant with boys from the youth program. One by one, in tones as sober as any of the judges who had once sentenced them, the men talked about their lives, their mistakes, the misery of prison, the even harder misery of realizing you've failed those who once cared, who once tried to help you.

The first snicker out of any of the boys, the first bored look or smart-ass remark, was the signal for a torrent of verbal abuse from the men who could go on for ten minutes at a clip. Very few teenagers were able to defy such an assault and Sean was no exception. His initiation into Hell Night came early, when Billboard jerked him aside for smirking and explained to him in graphic language just what would happen to a fine-figured wisp of a boy like him five minutes after he walked onto the cell block in a place like Arcadia.

That outburst was enough to get Sean's attention. After that, Billboard was able to lower the decibel level and tell his life story in drips and drabs, coaxing out the boy's own story in the process.

The second thing that helped turn Sean Carpenter around was the computer, an older donated IBM PC, in the church's rec room. The rec room had half a dozen distractions for the boys—two pool tables, ping-pong, air hockey, video games—but it was that old computer, with its minuscule 500K hard drive and its clunky modem, that drew Sean like a puppy to an old pair of slippers. It didn't take long, a matter of a few weeks, before Father Joe and everyone else involved in the program could see that the boy was a natural, a keyboard wizard. After a few months in the Y.O.P., Sean was helping out in the church office, showing the secretaries how to do bulk mailing lists or how to use a template of his own design to put together the weekly bulletin. By the end of his two-year commitment to the program, he was devising custom spreadsheets and budgeting software for Father Joe's entire operation. And, thanks to intensive tutoring, he had gotten himself back on track with his schoolwork and seemed ready to return to regular high school classes.

But there was one great worry for Father Joe and for Sean, as he turned seventeen and prepared to leave Corpus Christi's sheltering shadow. The streets of the city were still out there, and so were the Backus Avenue Boys.

"They wanted him back in the fold. You remember, Sister," said Father Joe, as he paced in front of his office window. "That kid Marco, Marco Pilato. How he started coming around looking for Sean, particularly after he found out about Sean's computing skills."

"Yes, I remember. I suppose Marco had thought up some way to exploit those skills—illegally, of course."

"And Sean wasn't immune to Marco's flattery, either. I think he knew that himself. He was reluctant at first when I suggested the abbey option, but he understood it was the best thing for him." Father Joe shook his head. "Dear Lord, how could I have known it would turn out like this?"

"You couldn't," Sister Matty said. "From what you've told me so far, it sounds as if the authorities down there don't know themselves what happened yet. Sean is merely a convenient suspect—"

"Convenient!" The priest threw up his hands. "I should

say so. He's run off, Sister, gone from the Witoviaks' home. And Brother John—poor Brother John. He was killed with a knife! You know how that all looks?"

Sister Matty leaned back and sighed. It certainly didn't look good.

A year earlier, as Sean turned seventeen and was preparing to leave the youth program, Father Joe had made a proposal. To get Sean out of the city and away from the lure of the Back Boys, Father Joe had made arrangements for him to move south to a new foster family in Garfield, a small town in Lorret County. There, he would complete his senior year at the local high school. In his free time he would work at the Abbey of the Ganannoqua and receive counseling from an old friend and mentor of Father Joe's, Brother John Kolumus.

"He's a crusty old monk with a Jesuit's wit and intelligence, but he's a bit set in his ways," Father Joe had told Sean.

Sean was reluctant to go until Father Joe mentioned the bakery operation and Brother John's role as the business manager. "He needs bringing into the computer age, Sean. They're barely removed from the abacus down there, I'm told."

*Computer* was the magic word, as Father Joe knew it would be. Sean agreed to move south for the year and to put himself in service to Brother John. From their letters, Father Joe followed the progress of the relationship and knew that it had been difficult from the beginning. But things had worked out; Sean had completed high school and had continued his work at the abbey right on into the summer. He was even planning to enter the Riverton University of Technology in the fall to study software engineering. He would receive financial help from the abbey's scholarship fund.

And now this. Brother John murdered and young Sean Carpenter missing.

Father Joe stopped pacing and stood behind his swivel chair, grasping its back with both hands as if to hold himself up.

"I've never felt so—helpless." With his red beard and the anguish etching deep lines onto his face, the golden backlighting from the windows behind him, he reminded Sister Matty of those tortured self-portraits by Vincent van Gogh. "I have to do something. Brother John is dead, and Sean is out there somewhere, apparently on the run. I can't stay here and go on as if nothing's happened."

The diminutive nun searched her brain for something constructive to say. She had worked with Father Costello for nearly a decade. He was a man who lived his Christianity every day and who suffered each parishioner's failure as if it were his own. She couldn't keep Joseph Costello from taking on the worries of the world, but she could help him carry the load.

"The first thing you should do," she suggested, "is talk to the sergeants. Find out what they think, where the investigation will go from here. If there's anything we can do ourselves to bring Sean in."

"Yes. I should've thought of that myself. That's good, Matty." He reached for the phone on the desk. "Maybe the sergeants can point me in the right direction anyway."

"And it's Thursday," she reminded him. "They're still serving late lunches at the cafe."

"Right again." He withdrew his hand from the phone. "Let's go see if Sergeant Hafner is having the usual today, shall we?"

# CHAPTER 4

"Ah, that hits the spot."

Sergeant Hafner was seated at his favorite table, near one of the tall narrow windows and below the framed poster of Burt Lancaster from *Birdman of Alcatraz*. The remains of the Thursday special, a Yardbird Chicken Club Sandwich with a side of Death Row Fries and a cup of the soup du jour, were on the table in front of him. At the seat opposite sat his partner of seven years on Riverton's Metro force, Sergeant Kelvin Greene. He was finishing up a plate of Big House barbecued baby-back ribs, wiping his fingers with the moist cloth that came with every order, careful to keep any of the spicy sauce from dripping onto his suit.

He had on a tan summer-weight two-piece outfit that day, with a pale yellow shirt and a silk paisley tie— a combination that showed well against the deep brown of his skin. Hafner was wearing his usual dark blue suit, one of two almost identical outfits that he wore

25

interchangeably throughout the year. "Clothes don't make the man," he liked to tell Greene, to which Greene invariably replied, "Good thing."

Despite their differences in age, in race and habits, even in their approaches to the work, they somehow added up to a good combination, like Chinese sweet-and-sour or a twilight doubleheader.

Hafner pushed away his plate and looked up at the man standing next to the table. "The only thing missing, padre," he said, barely suppressing a belch, "is a cold bottle of beer, huh, Kel?"

"And I'm afraid it will continue to be missing," Father Joe said, "so long as this place is part of our prison outreach." He did a little immediate outreach of his own, stretching across the table to take the check. "This one's on the house, gentlemen."

"Thanks, Father." Greene's eyebrows made arches. "What's the occasion?"

"I, uh, need some professional advice. A few minutes of your time—"

"Sure. Grab a chair."

Father Joe hesitated, glanced around the dining room. Since converting the restaurant to a prison theme, business had boomed. All it had taken was a few fake bars painted onto the windows, some framed movie posters from popular prison flicks on the walls, a sound system heavy with jailhouse music—Johnny Cash was just then rumbling out a rendition of "Folsom Prison Blues"—and the parolees themselves serving as waiters, busboys, and cooks.

Office people from midtown, along with east-side businesspeople and factory workers, had nearly filled the place every working day since. The largest crowds came for lunch. But it was two o'clock, and the dining room was emptying out, promising them a measure of privacy.

Father Joe took the offered chair and, prefaced by a deep breath, plunged into the story of Sean Carpenter and the Backus Avenue Boys and the Youth Outreach Program and Brother John. He laid himself bare like a penitent who'd been too long away from the confessional.

"Oh, man," Sergeant Greene said, shaking his head. "This monk was killed with a knife? That doesn't look good for your boy, Father."

"Not good at all," Hafner agreed. "Given the history of the Back Boys."

"I know, I know."

The Backus Avenue Boys had two defining characteristics: their red nylon jackets with the interlocking BBB on the back and the fact that they always carried knives, never guns. The reasoning supposedly was that possession of a knife was only a Class-C felony, whereas possession of a gun was a Class-A felony with a mandatory sentence.

"The cops down there got any physical evidence tying the kid to the murder?" Hafner asked.

"I—don't know. All the abbot told me—all that I remember, anyway—is that Brother John was stabbed to death and that Sean is wanted for questioning, but he has disappeared from his foster home."

"He rabbited, huh?" Hafner looked at his partner, who nodded in return. Both men knew what that meant. "We should be hearing from the investigators down in Lorret County anytime now, assuming they haven't found the kid."

"You?"

"Well, the department anyway. I don't know that it'll be me and Kel here."

Greene said, "When a suspect runs, ninety-nine out of a hundred head to wherever they call home, Father. The sheriff's department down there will no doubt call up here and request assistance in locating your boy."

"But you're with the Physical Crimes Unit. Surely they'll contact the Juvenile Division on this."

Hafner barked a laugh. "You're dreaming, padre. This kid of yours is what, seventeen or eighteen now? Wanted for questioning on a murder? He's graduated from the juvie division, believe me. We get a request from Lorret County, we'll get a BOL out on him. Maybe even assign a couple of suits to knock on a few doors over in his old neighborhood if we can spare the manpower—which we can't. Sooner or later he'll get tired of crashing in somebody's basement and he'll go down to the corner store for a pack of smokes and a cold forty-ouncer and that's when one of the cruisers'll spot him. After that, it's just a matter of corraling him."

Father Joe tugged nervously at the short hairs of his beard. "Corraling him. I don't think I like the implications of that, Sergeant. They wouldn't use armed force—?"

"Not if the kid doesn't provoke it. But let's remember something. This kid is a member of a violent gang—"

"Ex-member," Father Joe corrected. "What I think I'm hearing is that it would be much better all around if Sean surrendered himself for questioning, rather than leave it for the police to bring him in."

"That's always the smartest option," Greene said.

"I suppose I could try to locate Sean myself, talk him into coming in—"

"If you do, better take a couple of your ex-cons with you, padre. The kid lives up in Back Boy turf, remember?

They don't like people messing with their members, ex or otherwise."

"Yes, that's a good point. And could I ask you two to keep an eye out for the request when it comes in from Lorret County? Perhaps handle it yourselves—?"

"It doesn't work like that, Father. There's a rotation system in place for non-emergency requests," Greene explained. Seeing the pleading look on the priest's face, he added, "But—we'll do what we can for whatever that's worth."

"Well, thank you, gentlemen. You've been a great help, as always." He started to rise, then settled back onto his chair. "One other question. I'll be going down to the abbey myself as soon as the funeral arrangements are set, either tomorrow or Saturday. When I talk with the investigating officer down there—"

"You're planning on talking with the investigating officer?" Hafner asked. Then, "Why this should surprise me, I have no idea."

"I think I can provide some insight he won't be able to get anywhere else," Father Joe said. "And maybe, in the process, I can convince him not to concentrate all his energies on Sean as the sole suspect."

"Good luck," Hafner said. "From what you've told us, this kid's the perfect suspect. A criminal background, no long-term connection to the community down there— he's not even from Lorret County. Evidence or no evidence, getting the cops down there to let go of your boy as a suspect is gonna be like convincing a hungry pit bull to spit out a pork chop."

"Mm, I was afraid of that. I was wondering, do you know this man who's investigating for the sheriff's department down in Lorret County? His name, I'm told, is Podesta."

Neither detective knew the name.

"But I can give you one piece of advice when you approach him, padre," Hafner said. "All police organizations are political, okay? But the smaller the department, the more political they are. Up here, we're large enough so that most of the bullshit, you should excuse my French, filters down about to the captain level, then gets diluted. But with your rural cops, some sheriff with a twenty-, thirty-man force, everybody's under the microscope. Like, you can bet the farm that every last man on the Lorret County payroll, down to the rawest deputy, is a registered Republican, civil service or no civil service. Up here in the city, of course, it's automatic Democrats, but like I say, that's like at the captain level and above."

"What Harold's trying to tell you, Father," said Greene, "is don't be afraid to be aggressive and drop a few names when you're dealing with the cops down there. If you've got any juice in Lorret County, use it. If you don't, fake it."

# CHAPTER
# 5

Nobody had to convince Sergeant Podesta it was all about politics. And *being* politic. If it wasn't, he'd just as soon reach across the table and grab the old, dried-up monk by his scrawny neck and choke a few answers out of him.

If his anger showed, it didn't bother Brother Jerome. The man's expression, hidden behind a beard that reminded Podesta of an exploded mattress, remained as calm as the waters of the pond that could be seen in the distance through the window of the abbey library. He was all of five feet tall, this ancient holy man, with ruddy cheeks, a long red nose, and a shiny bald head. He'd make a perfect Sneezy, Podesta thought, if this were a production of *Snow White* instead of a murder investigation.

"This here is a list of questions, okay?"

"You don't have to shout at him, Sergeant," the abbot said mildly. He was seated at the head of the reading table, acting as an interpreter, more or less. Turns out not only would the hermit monk not speak to Podesta, he didn't want to listen to him, either. Father Mazewski was there to relay, in sign, the policeman's instructions. "Please, if you could just address your comments to me, I'll see that he understands."

"Oh, he understands, all right," Podesta muttered. He pushed the list across the trestle table. "Look, tell him I need answers to these ASAP, okay? So, please, whatever he's doing down in that fruit cellar of his, have him put it off a day."

"It's an old root cellar, Sergeant. And what Brother Jerome was doing when we called on him this morning is called in the Latin *lectio divina*. It means sacred reading, and it's at the heart of what we do here at the abbey. To disturb *lectio*, for any reason, is considered a serious matter."

Podesta, unimpressed, said, "What he was doing this morning was sitting in the mouth of that cave of his, staring at a lightning-struck cottonwood tree."

"Precisely." The abbot steepled his long fingers again, which was starting to bug Podesta more than the silent monk. "Sacred reading means a careful, continual, highly deliberate pondering of the Word of God. Most assume this means through Scripture alone, but it does not. God is in all things, after all—a piece of architecture, or a stained glass window, even in a damaged cottonwood tree, which is why Brother Jerome is pondering it."

"And how much longer, would you think, will he be pondering it?"

"It's hard to say. He always spends an hour or so in the morning and another hour or so in the afternoon, studying the cottonwood or other aspects of the grotto." The abbot shrugged under his loose habit. "It could be days or weeks that he devotes to a given object of interest. Months, even. It takes however long it takes."

Podesta gave up. He had the abbot pass along, through sign language, a few more instructions for Brother Jerome, then dismissed him. The old hermit took the pages of questions and left the library without ever having acknowledged the policeman's existence.

"Please don't take it personally, Sergeant," Father Mazewski said, reading the other man's frustration. "Brother Jerome loves you as he loves all mankind. But God takes precedence."

"Right." Podesta shuffled his notes and cleared his throat. He could do with a smoke, but that wasn't allowed anyplace on the abbey grounds. Earlier he'd driven back into town behind the coroner's wagon, as much to have a few cigarettes as to get briefed on the preliminary examination of the body. Now it was well into the afternoon, he'd been interviewing monastery personnel for hours, and he wanted a good stiff belt and a cancer stick so bad he was losing his concentration.

It didn't help that half his brain was thinking about Sean Carpenter, wondering what luck Trabold was having chasing the kid down. Father Mazewski had told him about the kid's background, and how he and Brother John worked together on the abbey's new computer. When he mentioned there had been trouble in their relationship since day one, Podesta had sent some uniforms into Garfield to pick up the boy at the foster home, only to find he'd taken off.

With that news, Podesta had moved Sean Carpenter to the head of his list of suspects. Matter of fact, he was the only name on the list so far. Now there was the problem of establishing motive. "A personality conflict," as the good abbot had characterized it, normally wasn't enough in itself to move someone to murder. The case looked a lot stronger if Podesta could show that there was a catalyst of some kind: something—or someone—that provoked the kid to resort to violence.

"Uh—yeah, this other hermit you told me about earlier, Father. Brother Chan? Lives farther out in the woods someplace?"

"Yes. He has a shack out beyond Beaver Pond."

Podesta was beginning to lose track of all the ponds too. There had to be half a dozen of them, including Mary's Pond down by the grotto, and the one he could see from the library window—he didn't know what that one was called. Now Beaver Pond.

"Where's that from here?"

"Well, you take the path east of the bakery turnaround and follow it down past the apple orchard, then out through the woods there for about another half mile."

"A half mile?"

"There are over twenty-five hundred acres here, Sergeant. The abbey itself is just the tip of the iceberg. There're woods, ponds, the grotto, contemplation paths, all the cultivated fields and orchards, and rolling hills."

"Yeah. Quite a place." You could turn the whole thing into a golf course if he had a say. "So why haven't I seen Brother Chan yet?"

"I don't know. I expect his duties have kept him away. Was there anything in particular you wanted to know—?"

"You did tell me he was the one who probably disapproved the most of your bakery operation. And he was dead set against any plans to expand, isn't that right?"

"Well, yes, Brother Chan is, shall I say, unwavering in his devotion to our vocation here at the monastery. He opposes anything that goes beyond the barest effort to survive, which is one of the reasons he chooses to isolate himself in the woods. But I never meant to suggest that Chan would ever use violence to promote his views."

"I just need to ask him some routine questions, like with the others. This one does talk, doesn't he?"

"Yes. In fact, when the mood strikes him, he can be quite a chatterbox."

"Great. Let's go see if we can find—"

"Um, excuse me, Father Mazewski."

"Ah, Walter. Come in, please." The abbot rose from the table and motioned the man lingering in the library doorway to enter, but he hung back a moment longer. "It's all right, Walter. This is Sergeant Podesta. He's investigating poor Brother John's death."

"Yes, I heard. I was down in Danport this morning calling on some local suppliers when the secretary at the home office reached me with the news. I was just— stunned, Father. I drove straight back up here."

"We appreciate that, Walter."

"I thought, well, as John's friend and business contact, I thought I should be here. To help in any way I can."

He was a large man, filling the doorway with his bulk, and he had a voice to match: deep and resonant, like a bassoon echoing inside an empty concert hall. But like some big men who had never come to terms with their size, there was a shyness about him. Almost a daintiness, which expressed itself in the way he now came across the room, slightly bowed, and offered his soft hand to Podesta.

"Walter Monday, Sergeant. I'm a resource agent for Wager's. A buyer. We have the exclusive contract to buy all the abbey's bread for our stores."

"I guess that figures," Podesta said.

Wager's was the largest supermarket chain in that part of the state. Anyone within the five-county Riverton metropolitan area who ate food was familiar with Wager's. The stores, particularly the chain's superstores, had practically coined the phrase "one-stop shopping." A typical Wager's superstore featured a pharmacy, video-rental shop and flower shop, a film processing center, a bakery, seafood counter, meat counter, health food and bulk food departments, a frozen food section the size of a hockey rink, and, in case you should get hungry amidst all that plenty, a food court featuring a pizza stand, a salad bar, and a submarine shop.

Podesta was tired of looking up at the man. He motioned Monday into the seat that Brother Jerome had just vacated, which was a little like exchanging a Chihuahua for a St. Bernard. Monday lowered himself into the chair with all the caution of a lunar module touching down on the moon.

The sergeant wasted no time with preliminaries. "I understand from the abbot here that Brother John was pushing to increase bread production. What can you tell me about that?"

"Yes, well, he was, um, exploring the idea on my behalf. That is, on Wager's behalf." The big man had bushy eyebrows and baleful brown eyes that seemed a bit small for the rest of him. "Y'see, we're expanding into the southern part of the state with a new superstore down in Danport—a hundred-twenty-thousand square feet of retail space to fill—and we'd naturally like to offer Thy Daily Bread to our new customers downstate. But that would mean the abbey bakery would have to increase its output. So I asked John to see how everyone here—" A nod to Father Mazewski. "—would feel about going to a full bake on Thursdays. That increase of about ten thousand loaves per week would give us the margin we need for our downstate expansion plans."

"Uh-huh." Podesta scribbled a note in his pad. "You know Brother Chan?"

"Oh yes. We've—I was going to say 'spoken' on a few occasions, but 'had words' is more like it. Brother Chan doesn't like me."

The abbot felt compelled to say, "It's not that he doesn't like you, Walt. He simply disapproves of what you do for us. He also disapproves of me and of any of us who think Thy Daily Bread is a good idea. You shouldn't take it personally."

"I just think he disapproves of me more than the rest."

"And maybe he disapproves of Brother John too?" Podesta suggested.

Monday cocked his large head to the side. "You're not thinking Brother Chan had anything to do with this tragedy? Because, I mean, that's just very, very difficult to believe, Sergeant. If you knew these men like I do—"

"But I don't. That's the point, isn't it?"

"Well, I suppose it is. But, honestly, despite our differences, I can't picture Brother Chan, or any of the brothers, lifting a hand against Brother John."

"How about getting someone else to do the dirty work for him? Like this kid who was working for Brother John—this Sean Carpenter? I understand Brother Chan was about the only monk the kid got along with."

"If that's true," Monday said, looking to Father Mazewski, "it has to be a case of opposites attracting."

"Well put," the abbot nodded. "But it is a fact that Sean and Brother Chan seemed to get along well, despite their differences. Where Sean is all gungho for new technologies and science, Chan is very much a traditionalist—a Luddite, almost, in terms of technology and all it implies. However, Chan has always been drawn to young people. He's our novice master, you know—in charge of overseeing the progress of our novices. And he's outgoing when he wants to be. I suspect the two enjoyed discussing their differences, whereas with Sean and Brother John everything came out as a conflict."

He cast a steely eye at Podesta. "What I do *not* suspect, Sergeant, is that somehow Chan would use Sean to attack Brother John. It's ridiculous."

"I'm just trying to get to the bottom of this murder, Father, okay? I gotta look at every possibility, from every angle, before I reject anything."

"Um, you know, Sean is the reason I came by," Walter Monday said. "I mean, he's one of the reasons. I thought I should tell you about what Brother John told me. Only it didn't have anything to do with Brother Chan that I can see—"

Podesta cut in. "What did Brother John tell you?"

"That, um, Sean is a Satanist."

Podesta shot forward. "A Satanist? You mean a devil worshiper? Why did he think that?"

"It had to do with the Internet," Monday said, a bit flustered by the policeman's intensity. "I'm not really up on computers any more than necessary to do my job and file orders and such. But John told me that he'd caught Sean using the new computer in the bakery office to connect with various Web sites. These Web sites were all either pornography or Satanic groups."

To his left, Podesta heard the abbot let out a sigh, but he kept his eyes glued on the big man across the table. "What else did Brother John tell you? And when did this all happen?"

"Well, it happened just yesterday, Wednesday, when I came by to see that things were going smoothly, as I usually do on one of the full-bake days. Keeping a close personal relationship with your suppliers is key in the food marketing business." He took a cotton handkerchief from the pocket of his suitcoat and wiped his brow. "Warm in here today, isn't it?"

Podesta just stared at him.

"Well, anyway, John told me he and Sean had words before about inappropriate use of the Internet connection, and he planned on having it out with him once and for all. I told him that, frankly, it just sounded like typical kid stuff. I mean, a teenage boy looking at porno is pretty standard. Even the Satan stuff—don't they get that sort of thing from all that heavy metal music?"

"What did Brother John have to say to that?"

"He said that what went on out in the secular world was beyond his reach, but that this sort of thing couldn't be allowed to happen inside the abbey. It was the worst sort of blasphemy, he told me. He really was, um, quite worked up about it."

"I can imagine." Podesta wrote a few shorthand notes in his pad. He asked Walter Monday a few more questions, but he was pumping a dry well; the bread buyer had told all he could tell about the Internet incident. Podesta thanked him for coming and watched the big man leave the library, bringing to mind the dancing hippos in that weird old Disney cartoon. What was it, *Fantasia*?

"Of course, Sergeant," the abbot was saying, "despite how it sounds, this doesn't necessarily mean Sean Carpenter killed Brother John."

"No," Podesta conceded. "It only gives him a viable motive." He thought a few moments before asking, "You knew about the Internet stuff, didn't you, Father?"

The abbot took a few moments himself before answering. "Yes. About the pornography only. Brother John came to me for counsel a few weeks ago, when he first discovered Sean was using the computer in that way."

"And?"

"And I advised he lay the law down to the boy. Let him know we wouldn't tolerate such behavior in the future. I know he spoke to Sean, and I'd assumed the problem was ended." He frowned, drawing deep lines into his lean face. "I understand Walter's 'boys will be boys' assessment, but a monastery has a special relationship to God. Or we hope we do. This isn't something we could tolerate. And now, to hear Sean not only ignored an earlier warning, but also began accessing Satanic Web sites—"

"So why didn't you eliminate the problem by eliminating the kid? Or the Internet connection?"

"Because both are helpful to us in what we do here. We have our own Web site now, you know. It helps connect us to the outside world, to let those interested in helping know about our missions in Africa and Latin America, about various of our brothers' writings, about spiritual conferences and retreats. It's invaluable, giving us instantaneous worldwide exposure without our ever having to leave the abbey."

"And the kid," Podesta said. "I guess he was invaluable because he's the one who knew how to work the Web site?"

The abbot turned up his palms. "He designed it for us."

"Figures." Podesta nodded as he flipped shut his notepad. "Well, what say we go find Brother Chan now?"

# CHAPTER 6

"Yes, Father Costello, we got the request from Lorret County this morning." Hafner shifted the phone to his other ear, freeing up his right hand to work the wax paper on his sandwich. "No, not me personally. It got assigned to the uniform division for now. . . . No, not what you'd call a high priority."

Spread out across the desk were the usual jumble of incident reports, prelims from the M.E.'s office, miscellaneous case files, and a four-color brochure from Monahan's RV and Travel Trailer Jamboree out on Rte. 99. The sergeant was careful to move the brochure to one side, so as not to drip any mayo on it.

"The thing is, padre, we're up to our eyeballs in open cases right now or I'd volunteer to go up to the north side and poke around myself. . . . Uh-huh. . . . Uh-huh. You betcha, Father. I hear anything, I'll give you a call. . . . Okay, then."

Hafner returned the phone to its cradle and returned his attentions to his sandwich and his RV dreams, but the reverie didn't last long. It was 12:33 P.M. on Friday when most of the detectives in the Physical Crimes Unit, including Greene, were off eating lunch somewhere fancy. Hafner, as was his usual practice, had brown-bagged it. Only on Thursday afternoons, when The Hard Time Cafe ran its blue-plate specials, did he give in to his partner's needling and go out for lunch. As he had told Greene, he had to save up for that new recreational vehicle.

But on this particular noon hour, his frugality cost him in other ways.

Lieutenant Garafino dropped a phone slip into the pile on the desk. "Down the block at the A-OK parking lot, the one by the river? You've got a thirteen, fresh; the blood hasn't even coagulated on the pavement."

"Why me? Oh, shit," Hafner whined as, despite his foresight, mayonnaise dripped from his chicken patty sandwich onto a corner of the four-color brochure. "Greene and me've got the biggest case load in the squad as it is."

"Because," answered the lieutenant with a pitiless grin and a glance around the empty squad room, "like the man told the hooker, your desirability is surpassed only by your availability."

"Ha, ha. You're a regular Steinfeld, Loo."

"That's *Sein*feld, no *t*." Garafino tapped the phone slip. "The other reason is this victim was gunned down next to his RV. I figure that's right up your alley, Harold."

Hafner didn't say anything else because there was no point. He'd been caught red-handed with the brochure in plain sight on his desk. Besides, the lieutenant was already on the way back to his cubicle to handle the next item on his action list. Hafner snatched up the phone slip, read it over quickly, then rewrapped the chicken sandwich in wax paper and shoved it back into the bag.

*       *       *

The victim was, indeed, lying in a heap next to a recreational vehicle parked in a double spot at the rear-left corner of the A-OK lot. The RV in question, Hafner couldn't help noticing, was a Winnebago Warrior, twenty-two feet long, almost new, dark blue with beige trim. A nice rig for a couple or maybe a small family, he acknowledged. He himself owned a twenty-four foot Mallard, which was okay for a family of four like his, but he had his eye on a Coachman Mirada that was pure class. If only he could convince Marie . . .

It was with considerable reluctance that the sergeant shifted his sightline down from the big blue camper to the victim. Yuck, a bleeder. Got it in the pump, it looked like, blood all over the tarmac, already drying toward dark brown. That unmistakable copper smell still hung in the humid air, though.

The victim was a man in his late forties, full head of brown hair silvering around the temples, long narrow nose and face. Dull brown eyes opened wide in perpetual shock.

*Well sure*, Hafner thought. *Nobody's ever ready to die violently and suddenly.* He'd seen the look on dozens of the dead, even death row inmates who knew what was coming. Maybe we just never believe in our own mortality, deep down, until death forces the issue.

This victim was most likely a businessman. It didn't take an experienced detective to figure out that much, given the three-piece suit and the parking lot close to the financial district. Hafner glanced up, taking in the high-rise office buildings that crowded the surrounding blocks, leaving the lot almost entirely shaded even at that early afternoon hour.

"We got an ID yet?" he asked.

"Muncy. Alan Everett Muncy," said the patrol officer who'd been first on the scene. "Got it from the guy in the shack, the attendant, some kinda Arab. Muncy, like in Indiana, only this one's spelled with a *y*."

"Everybody's gotta be different," Hafner said. "The attendant still in the shack?"

"Yeah. Says he didn't see nothin', don't know nothin'." The uniform crouched. "Don't look like a mugging, Sarge. Guy's still got his rings and watch, and I'd bet that bulge there is a wallet."

"Yeah, well, we'll see."

\*    \*    \*

The attendant was a slim, brown young man whose name, if Hafner caught it right, was Fudd.

"Like Elmer?" he asked him, speaking too loud. "Fudd?"

"No, not Elmer. Osmani." The kid pointed to himself and smiled. "Call me Ozzie. Ozzie Faud—F-A-U-D."

"Ahh." Hafner wrote it down, wondering in the back of his mind where all these Third-Worlders seem to come up with such pearly white teeth. "So, Ozzie, what happened out here anyway?"

The hands started moving—pointing, swooping, waving—in harmony with the heavily accented boarding-school English. A lot of energy the kid was putting into it but, boiled down, he hadn't seen a thing, hadn't heard a thing, didn't know a thing.

"How about Muncy? You know him when you see him?"

"Oh, yes, naturally." The hands went again, motioning back toward the Winnebago, which towered over everything else on the lot. "Every morning I must guide Mr. Muncy into his special slot, off the side street there. Seven-forty-five each morning. Weekdays only."

"He drives the RV to work on a regular basis?" Hafner asked.

"Oh, yes. He pays double the monthly rate. Visa gold card."

"Right. Visa gold card. And he parks for the day, huh? He works in one of these office buildings?"

Osmani Faud agreed that Mr. Muncy did, indeed, work in one of the nearby office buildings, only he had no idea which one.

"You're not a real observant fella, are you there, Ozzie?"

"I observe the cars that come in and the cars that go out. I make certain that everyone has paid." He shrugged, his shoulders about as thick as a wire coat hanger inside his regulation green A-OK parking lot attendant's shirt. "That is my job. I see cars, not people."

Hafner pursed his lips and exhaled. It was stuffy in there, even just standing in the doorway of the shack. How anyone could sit in there all day, every day, sucking exhaust fumes into his lungs, was beyond Hafner's understanding.

"So," he said, "was it usual for the victim—Mr. Muncy—to come down to his RV at the lunch hour?"

The kid blinked, then frowned, then shrugged and smiled. "I'm sure I wouldn't know that, sir."

"Well, did you ever see him come down to the RV in the middle of the day?"

"I can't say that I ever saw him, and I can't say that I ever didn't see him. You see?"

Maybe the fumes had gone to the kid's head. "No, I don't see, Oz."

"As I said, I see cars—"

"Not people." Sergeant Hafner's stomach let go a long, low growl.

# CHAPTER 7

W anda Witoviak was a thin wisp of woman, frail and shy. In her flowery shift, low-heeled loafers, and simple gold chain and crucifix, she might have been on her way to Mass, or to visit a sick friend, or perhaps off for a bit of shopping at the mall in Victorville. But no, she had assured Father Costello when he came by. He was interrupting no plans of hers, other than to carry on with her usual household duties.

"And worrying about Sean," she added, coloring slightly. "I guess, one way or another, I've worried about them all over the years. As if they were my own."

This last was a well-worn phrase for her. She was forty years old and barren, a hateful word that she never used but which was often in her thoughts. It didn't help that George, her husband, was constantly explaining their childlessness to people with his own well-worn phrase: "Wanda can't have kids." He didn't do it to be cruel, of

46

course—merely to take any responsibility from himself. It was the one flaw, among the many small imperfections within their marriage, for which she'd never quite been able to forgive him.

Becoming foster parents had been George's idea. She'd been reluctant at first, fearful even, at the thought of opening her home to strangers. But the children had soon changed her mind. "They give me something to work at every day, someone to care about besides myself. You wouldn't understand how important that is, Father, but then you're not stuck in a big empty house in a little bitty town with nothing but the telephone and *Oprah* to keep you company."

But Father Costello did understand. He, too, lived in a big empty house and often felt the loneliness and the isolation of it. Perhaps that's one of the reasons he poured so much energy into the church's outreach programs; the participants were the closest thing to family he would ever have.

The Witoviaks had taken in five children in the past seven years, Wanda told him. Right now there was Tiffany, a seven-year-old girl who had been removed from her mother's home by county social workers. She was attending a birthday party down the street that afternoon. And then there was Sean Carpenter. Sean was, by several years, the oldest of the children the Witoviaks had taken in. Up until now, she told Father Costello, they'd had no reason to regret the decision.

"I still don't regret it, Father, but George—well, he's got the business to think about. Public opinion counts, he says, even if you're just running a small-town hardware store."

Father Costello nodded neutrally. They were having coffee in the Witoviaks' family room, seated carefully on cream-colored leather furniture that was too soft and felt cold to his touch. The house was a neat center-entrance colonial on one of Garfield's nicest residential streets, with a large yard that featured, in back, a colorful swing set.

He'd decided to drive down that afternoon, even though the services for Brother John wouldn't be held until the next day, Saturday. Father Joe planned to spend the night at the abbey, finding out whatever he could about Brother John and Sean and what could've gone wrong between them. The visit to the Witoviaks' home was a courtesy as much as anything. It had been his request, through the diocese's Catholic Services, that had gotten Sean placed there. But he also had several questions he wanted to ask Wanda Witoviak. Her answers, alas, threw very little light on Brother John's death.

"So, Wanda, you don't know exactly when—or why—Sean disappeared?"

"All I know is that he didn't come down for breakfast yesterday morning, and when I checked his room, he wasn't there," she said, her index finger nervously rubbing at the side of her coffee cup. "The police have been here twice. They searched Sean's room. Don't ask me what they were after."

"Did Sean pack his things—?"

"No, not that I can tell. Oh, he may've taken a change of clothes and a few books. I can't really keep track. He didn't have that much to begin with. Oh, and his bike, of course. He went everywhere on that bike."

"You mentioned, when we spoke on the phone last night, that there were some other boys who came around to see Sean recently?"

"Yes, from the city. Two boys in an old, loud car, both of them wearing red jackets. I told the police about that too. I hope that's all right."

"Of course it is, Wanda. You have to cooperate with the authorities."

"That's what George said. I felt, I don't know, like I was betraying Sean in some way, telling that officer about him and his personal business." Her eyes widened as if she had just realized something. "It *is* a murder investigation, after all, so I guess I'm foolish to feel that way."

"These boys," Father Joe probed, "did you happen to learn from Sean what they wanted?"

"Not really. They came to the door one day, asking for Sean. I told them he was up at the monastery working. They left, then came back the next day when Sean was here." She added, "This was about a week ago, maybe ten days."

"Did you tell Sean about the boys' visit the first time, when they missed him?"

"Well, yes, I did, but he didn't really say much about it. I had the idea he already knew, like maybe they drove up to the monastery to find him. He didn't have a lot to say about any of this, except I'd say he was quieter than normal from that day on."

Father Costello sat back and concentrated for a few moments on his cup of coffee. Then he asked, "Wanda, is there anything else you can tell me that might shed some light on Sean's disappearance? Did he speak to you about any troubles he was having with Brother John, for example? Anything that could possibly make sense of all this?"

"No, I'm sorry, Father. Sean's a good boy, respectful and everything, but he doesn't really confide in me or in George, either. I guess if he talked about personal things with anyone, it'd be Mike Keller."

Mike Keller, she explained, was a friend of Sean's from

Garfield High. His only friend, it seemed. When Sean
arrived at the school the previous fall for his senior year, he
was seen as an outsider by most of the kids. He had a hard
time fitting in at first, making a place for himself, until one
of the teachers introduced him to the computer club.

"We don't have a home computer ourselves," Mrs.
Witoviak said. "The poor boy was bored to tears, I think,
until he joined that club. Then he spent just about every
extra hour there when he wasn't home sleeping and
eating or out to the monastery working. Mike was
president of the club, and I guess he's about the only one
who spent more time in the school's computer lab last
year than Sean did. They got to be pretty close."

\*    \*    \*

The Kellers lived on the outskirts of Garfield in a
sprawling ranch house set a hundred yards back from the
road and surrounded by cornfields. Father Costello had
no trouble finding the place, thanks to Wanda Witoviak's
directions and an oversized mailbox at the end of the
driveway that had KELLER printed on it. Mrs. Keller, a
petite blond with a comfortable smile, greeted him at the
door. Her son came out of his room long enough to be
introduced to the priest and to lead Father Joe back to
his room, firmly closing the door behind him.

"Parents," Mike Keller said, as if that were the only
explanation necessary.

Unlike Sean's spartan bedroom at the Witoviak home,
Mike Keller's room looked like something out of a NASA
training film. In addition to three different PCs with
monitors, there were two printers, a modem, something
that appeared to be a scanner, a phone, and a black box
with all sorts of wires running out the back like rope
licorice. The walls were papered with posters of rock
groups and science fiction films. Various bits of clothing

peeked out from under the bed, which looked as if it had been hastily made up moments earlier.

On second glance, Father Joe realized one of the machines he'd taken to be a PC was actually just a television set. "Nice place you've got here," he said, taking a seat on the bed.

"Yeah, well, it's okay. Your call kinda caught me by surprise. I mean, I didn't have time to, y'know, pick up much."

"I didn't realize how quick I'd be, driving over from the Witoviaks'."

"Yeah, it's not very far." At first, the boy didn't know what to do with himself, nervously moving his slight frame back and forth, like a monkey pacing its cage. He finally pulled the ladderback chair away from the desk where the newest and largest computer reigned supreme and sat himself down. He pushed his glasses up the bridge of his nose and sniffled. "So, um, I guess I call you Father, right? I mean, we're Lutherans, but it's not like we're regulars or anything."

Father Joe smiled. "Whatever makes you comfortable, Mike. I promise I won't keep you long anyway."

"It's okay. I'd like to help you if I can. Only, I don't really know anything."

"What about the two Backus Avenue Boys who came down to see Sean sometime last week? Did he tell you about that?"

"Yeah. He was kinda bummed about it, I think."

"How do you mean?"

"Like he was upset. In a way I think he missed some of the guys in his old gang, y'know? The friendships. Only these guys who came down here, they wanted him to go back to Riverton and work some kinda scam for 'em and

Sean wasn't into that anymore." Mike looked into the middle distance between them and shook his head. "It's like he was caught in between his old life with those gangbangers and the new life he was planning for himself, y'know? He talked about starting at Riverton Tech this fall, computer science, getting on with his life."

"I see. Is there anything else he told you about them? Did they threaten him?"

"Yeah, they might have. One was named Marco, he said, and I guess he's like the leader of the gang or whatever. I think Sean was afraid of him." He shrugged. "That's all he told me, really, that they wanted him back but he wasn't into it anymore."

"Okay. How about his work at the abbey? Did he talk about that or Brother John?"

"Oh, yeah, sometimes. Mostly he bitched about how old-fashioned the guy is and how pitiful the hardware is over there. They had him building a Web site on this wimpy two-thirty-three meg system with a crappy modem, which is almost as bad as the junk we have to use at school." He pointed to the computer behind him. "I put that baby together myself. Four-fifty megs and a six-gig drive. I could download the *Encyclopedia Britannica* if I wanted to and run Riven at the same time."

"Impressive," Father Joe said. He had only understood every other word, but it certainly had sounded impressive. "Mike, I'm trying to find out if there was anything going on with Brother John and Sean, anything that might've led Sean to attack Brother John."

"Hah! The other way around maybe," the boy blurted, then looked away.

"What's that mean, Mike? Sean did something that made Brother John angry?"

"You could say that, I guess."

He continued to keep his eyes averted, fiddling with the computer's keyboard.

"Anything you can tell me might help Sean, Mike. That's why I'm here."

The boy thought about it, the silence of the room stretching to a half a minute before he turned back to the priest. His cheeks reddened as he said, "Well, first off there was the porn thing."

"The porn thing?" Father Joe repeated.

Mike Keller told him about Sean using the abbey PC to access pornography Web sites and how Brother John "pretty much blew a gasket" when he caught him at it. Sean had been deeply embarrassed by the incident, according to Mike, and had promised never to do it again.

"And did he keep his word?"

"Far as I know."

"But there was something else, wasn't there?" Father Joe pressed, watching the boy's face. "You said *first* there was the porn."

"Well—" He frowned. "I don't think he wanted me to tell anyone about this."

"I'm on Sean's side, remember?"

"Yeah. He talked about you sometimes. Father Joe this and Father Joe that. Almost like you were his real father, y'know?"

Father Joe smiled. "Thank you. That's good to hear."

"Anyway, I don't know the details, but Sean told me he found something out about Brother John. That 'Mr. Holier-Than-Thou' wasn't as clean as he liked to pretend and that if Sean wanted to, he could take him down a peg. He told me that a few days ago. The last time I saw him, in fact."

"He didn't explain what he meant?"

"Nope. Sean was like that, having secrets or pretending to know stuff." Mike grinned ruefully. "You never know with him. Maybe he found out the monk was foolin' around with some kinky Web sites himself. Or maybe Sean was just making it up to take the sting out of being caught at it himself."

"Mmm." Father Joe stroked his beard. "I might agree with you except for the fact Brother John has been murdered and Sean has disappeared."

"Yeah." The boy hung his head. "I guess that means *something* was up, all right."

"One last question, Mike. Do you have any idea where Sean might be?"

He thought about it. "If I had to bet, I'd say probably he went back to the city, maybe even back to the Backus Avenue Boys. That makes the most sense, I guess. But y'know, sometimes me and Sean would sit in here and talk about stuff, how we'd love to be able to drive across the country in a convertible, all the way across the fruited plains and the purple mountains out to California. Hanging out in Silicon Valley with a juiced laptop in one hand and some golden blond in the other."

He turned bright red again. "Anyway, that's the version I'd *like* to believe."

# CHAPTER
## 8

At four o'clock that afternoon, just about the time Father Costello was leaving the Keller ranch house in Garfield, two of the men from his prison outreach program were walking some of Riverton's meaner streets. Reuben Macky was a large, bald-headed black man with bulging biceps. William Lee Ralston was a tall, slim white man with tattoos running wrist to shoulder on both muscle-corded arms. The pair cut a wide swath up the sidewalks of the Backus Avenue neighborhood.

"You know, of course, every badass in the hood already went underground," Macky said.

Ralston, known as Billboard by nearly everyone, said, "Don't matter. Joe wants us to look for the kid, we look."

Macky, a former burglar and stickup artist, was the operations manager at The Hard Time Cafe. Billboard, ex-biker and dope pusher, was its head chef. They were opposites in nearly every way, the former having grown up in an inner-city housing project like those surrounding them, while the latter was raised in downstate's rural hill country. They got along because of a shared experience—years locked away inside Arcadia State Penitentiary. And because of a common debt—neither wanted to disappoint the man who had given them a second chance.

"Goes without sayin', man. I'm just sayin' the word's out. The gangbangers aren't about to turn over one of their own, to us or the cops."

"He ain't one of theirs anymore."

"Then why the hell we lookin' for him all up and down this sorry-ass place?"

"What I'm sayin' is, if he had no place to run to, he might just end up back here on home turf. That don't mean he's back with the old crowd, doin' the old things, Macky. It only means his choices got real limited real fast."

"Uh-huh. I'll try to remember the distinction, hillbilly."

"You do that."

"And you keep in mind we gotta be back to work soon, and we got *no* choice about that."

They had been out for two hours, leaving the restaurant the minute the Friday lunch crowd thinned out enough to allow for a break. A city bus ride had brought them from Carson Avenue to the lower end of Backus Avenue on Riverton's north side. The job, as outlined by Father Joe, was to look for Sean Carpenter and, if possible, convince him to come back to Corpus Christi to give himself up to the police.

They had started their search in the tenement where Sean had lived with his junkie mother, a fourth-floor unit in the Harriet Tubman building of the Backus-Rose Community Apartment Towers. Despite the fancy name, it was a complex of subsidized high-rise apartment houses that resembled rows of ice cube trays set on end. Pitted, rusty ice cube trays that stank of twenty-five years of fried foods and urine and despair.

But the Tubman building, like the rest of the neighborhood, gave up no answers that day. It was like patrolling the jungle in Vietnam, Billboard told Macky— the silence and the heat everywhere but no people. And yet you knew they were out there, watching you, deciding whether it was better to let you go away or just to kill you.

"If you're tryin' to make me feel better," Macky said, "it ain't happening."

From the Backus-Rose project, they worked their way back over to the main street, stopping along the way at mom-and-pop stores, barber shops, gas stations— anyplace where a human face could be found and a question asked. But there were no answers forthcoming.

"A few more blocks, man," Billboard kept saying. "For Joe and the kid. A few more blocks."

\*     \*     \*

Back downriver at the Abbey of the Ganannoqua, Sergeant Podesta had at last succeeded in tracking down Brother Chan. At Chan's insistence, they sat down to talk in the woods surrounding the hermit's tiny shack.

Podesta was saying, "So if the kid was such a pain in the neck, always disagreeing with you on your religious beliefs, why'd you bother? I mean, why give him the time of day?"

"Tolerance," the monk said, his broad Eurasian face emotionless behind thick, black glasses. "A monk's calling is to live a humble life. Humble in our daily work and prayer, in the clothes we wear and the food we eat. Humble also in relation to our fellow man. We must remind ourselves not to feel superior to those we see as less pious. Do you see?"

"No, not really."

"Let me give you an example on a smaller scale. You use tobacco, Sergeant. I can smell it on your clothes. This is personally offensive to me. Our order forbids its use, you see, and smoking isn't allowed anywhere on abbey grounds."

"I haven't had a single cigarette on these grounds—"

"I wasn't accusing you. My point has to do with tolerance. I disapprove of the use of tobacco, and yet I accept in my presence a smoker. I *tolerate* you and your addiction because to do otherwise would be to *judge* you. It isn't the role of a humble man to be the judge of other men; that's God's business alone."

That little speech didn't sound too tolerant to Podesta, but he pushed on anyway. "So you built this friendship with Sean out of tolerance? Being a humble monk?"

"Yes." He paused, the suggestion of a smile passing across his lips. "And also because I'm a polemicist at heart, no doubt due to my Jesuit training." Sensing the other man's difficulty with the word, he added, "It means I enjoy discussing controversial subjects."

"I know what it means," Podesta lied. Sitting there on a fallen tree trunk, the rough bark pinching his ass while this smug Chinaman insulted his intelligence, made him feel as if he'd stepped into the middle of a really bad episode of *Kung Fu*. Time to cut to the chase.

"You expect me to believe you developed a close personal bond with this juvenile delinquent from the city because you got a kick out of arguing about God with an atheist?"

"What you believe is not my concern. But for the

record, Sean isn't an atheist; he's an agnostic. And agnosticism is something I not only can tolerate but, in some sense, admire."

Even though he was opening himself up for another sermon, Podesta couldn't resist saying, "You're gonna have to explain that to me."

Brother Chan crossed his arms inside the loose sleeves of his smock and seemed to rock back a bit, as if the tree trunk were as comfortable as a La-Z-Boy recliner. Podesta, meanwhile, squirmed to find a more comfortable position.

"I must make an admission here, Sergeant, that causes me some dismay. It is this: There is a belief which is shared equally by the pious and the profane alike. It is the acceptance of something which cannot be proven to be fact. On the one hand, believers have faith that God exists; on the other hand, atheists have a sort of faith, too, that He does *not* exist. You understand that *neither* position can be proven?"

"I see what you mean."

The hermit monk nodded approvingly, as if one of his novitiates had correctly answered a question about Revelations. "Only the agnostic has the intellectual honesty to admit that he does not know the answer to the unanswerable question. You see? The agnostic alone says, 'I can neither prove nor disprove God's existence; therefore, no matter how much I want to believe, I doubt.'"

It sounded to Podesta as if Brother Chan, the oh-so-pious hermit monk, was having a little crisis of faith himself. "And that's Sean Carpenter? Someone who wants to believe but can't quite summon up the faith?"

"I think so, yes. Certainly, he wants to believe in something. At first it was the gang he fell in with, and when that was taken away, it became science and technology. He put all his faith in machines and in man the innovator. When that, too, failed to give him the answers he was seeking—"

"Hold on." It was clear by the loss of his neutral expression that Chan wasn't used to being interrupted. That pleased Podesta. "You're saying the kid was disillusioned with computers and science all of a sudden?"

"Disillusioned? Hmm, that might be too strong—or perhaps it's not. I would say Sean is at least more open these days to the possibility that science doesn't hold all the answers to life. That man must look outside himself for some answers."

"Because of what? His talks with you?"

"Yes. With me and with Brother John and probably with some of the others as well. A young person with a bright, questioning mind can't spend a year working at a monastery and not have something rub off, after all. If that were the case, we'd all be dismal failures."

Podesta couldn't take any more. He slid off the trunk of the mossy old oak and flexed his hips like a hula dancer warming up. It felt as if someone were sticking pins in the cheeks of his ass.

"Since we're on the subject," he said. "I thought you and Brother John didn't get along."

"We have—we *had* fundamental disagreements over this abbey's mission, it's true," Chan said, choosing his words even more carefully than usual. "He believed in a much broader interpretation of our duties. I believe we are here to subsist and pray and pay homage to Christ only. John wanted to use our productive capacity more fully, so that we might extend our mission to other places and in other ways."

"I guess you opposed the idea of going to a full bake on Thursdays?"

"Naturally. If I had my way, we'd reduce from three days a week to two and sell only so much bread as it takes to live on from year to year. I'd get rid of all the fancy stainless steel equipment in the bakery as well and get back to doing it entirely by our own hands, good honest work, as Benedict and Christ would have it."

Money and religion, a potent mixture. Podesta raised an eyebrow. "Some might call that a motive to have Brother John killed."

Chan frowned ruefully and shook his head. "Sergeant, if I were about to be trampled to death by a rampaging elephant, I would do my best to step aside and thus save myself. But I wouldn't attempt to do harm to the animal, even if it were in my power. Because to do harm to one of God's creatures would betray everything I live my life for. The elephant, after all, is simply doing what an elephant does."

He pointed toward his shack, a poor, little wooden structure, perhaps ten feet by ten feet, containing a bed of boards and straw, a potbellied woodstove for heat, and little else.

"I live out here alone and attempt to commune with God as I believe we are intended to do—I get out of the beast's way. That is my answer to the elephant of commerce that threatens this abbey, Sergeant, and my answer to you."

Sergeant Podesta was a practical man; he knew when he was outclassed. He had one more question in him, however, and he went straight for the bottom line. "Do you know anything at all about Brother John's murder or Carpenter's disappearance?"

The hermit monk shook his head. "Nothing."

On the trudge back up the path to the abbey, Podesta tried to put Brother Chan away in a corner of his mind where he kept annoying bits of information. It was the same corner where he had earlier filed Brother Jerome. He let his mind wander over the case and ended up wondering how Deputy Trabold was doing in his search for the kid. He'd sent a request up to Riverton that morning, but it was too early to expect anything back. Still, it was a good bet that Carpenter had run back to familiar turf.

Trabold didn't like it—he was worried about losing the collar to the Riverton cops. But as far as Podesta was concerned, he'd be happy to ship them the whole damn case file, and good riddance.

*   *   *

Macky and Billboard were themselves about two minutes from calling it a day. One last block, Billboard had pleaded, and then they'd head back over to Backus Avenue and pick up a bus over to Carson.

"We're gonna be late as it is," Macky grumbled. "Chet and the others gonna be pissed if they gotta do all the setup themselves for the dinner crowd."

"Chet knows how to delegate the wait staff," Billboard said, "and I left good instructions for my boys in the kitchen. Besides, if we're already late, man, another twenty minutes ain't gonna matter anyhow."

"That's the kinda dumb-ass thinkin' got you incarcerated in the first place, hillbilly."

"Yeah, one cell block over from you, genius."

They were passing a boarded-up grocery store on Lemond Street. Suddenly, half a block ahead, two young men walked out of an alley, talking with their heads down and their hands moving. They were wearing identical red jackets.

Billboard had just enough time to slap Macky's arm

and say, "Hey, look!" before the pair saw them and quickly did an about-face back into the alley.

"Come on!" Billboard began sprinting down the cracked sidewalk with Reuben Macky reluctantly following. Turning into the alley, they could see the boys rounding a corner farther up, the linked BBB showing plainly on the backs of their red jackets. This was unfamiliar territory for the two ex-cons, a series of interconnecting alleyways that formed a maze between the old commercial strip along Lemond and a group of small industrial buildings, most of them shuttered now, that ran south and east for several blocks.

"Move it, Macky!" Billboard shouted over his shoulder. "Those punks are Backus Avenue Boys!"

"No shit?" Macky huffed. "I thought they was with the Better Business Bureau. Man, you are one dumb-ass peckerwood."

"Yeah, well, I got enough—"

Enough what, he didn't say. Because, as the men rounded another corner and plunged into the deep shadows of the looming buildings, they came face to face with the two boys they'd been chasing. And boys they were, no more than fifteen, Macky estimated.

"Hey," one of them called out. "What the hell you mu'fuckers want?"

Out of the side of his mouth, Macky said, "Kids say the darnedest things."

"We just wanna talk, is all." Billboard spread open his hands. "We're lookin' for somebody. An ex-Back Boy."

From behind them came another voice. "All *ex*-Back Boys are dead, asshole."

Macky and Billboard both turned halfway, enough to see the new threat while keeping the old one in view.

The new threat was worse: five more red jackets, these older and tougher looking. And showing knives.

Identical flick-knives with black bone handles and six-inch blades that gleamed even in the shaded alley. Five little Back Boys all in a row, blue-jeaned legs spread apart, knives casually at their sides, looking like some high school production of *West Side Story.*

"Hey, man," Macky said, "there's no need for the hardware."

"You guys know what we're after," Billboard said, not losing an inch of attitude. "Sean Carpenter. He used to run with you dudes—"

"I tole you, man, there ain't no *used to* with the Boys. Once you in, you in for life."

The speaker was a tall, well-built kid of maybe eighteen, dressed in his gang colors, a Nike T-shirt, a pair of jeans that looked ready to fall off, and hundred-dollar sneakers. He had red hair and fair skin and eyes as blue as the patch of sky high overhead. Under different circumstances, Macky would've laughed; it never failed to amaze him, how many white kids wanted to look and sound black. A couple of the others actually were black, along with a kid who looked Hispanic and another who was maybe Italian. *An equal-opportunity gang,* Macky thought wryly. *And they say this country ain't making racial strides.*

Billboard wouldn't give up. "Whatever you say, kid. We're just interested in talking to Sean, okay? Or maybe your leader, Marco Pilato, could help us out. We thought you guys could put us in touch with one or the other."

Macky let Billboard do the talking to the redhead. He was busy watching the others, in particular the stockier of the two black kids. He could see it in his face, in the way he played the knife blade back and forth across the

leg of his jeans like a barber stropping a razor. The little
bastard wanted to cut somebody.

"Yo, yo," the redhead said, "who says we know where
Sean is, man?"

"C'mon," Billboard said. "You guys know the cops want
him for questioning in a murder. Even if you boys don't
read the papers, it's all over the street." When there was
no response, he threw up his hands. "Hey, maybe he's
around, maybe he ain't. All's we're askin' is you let him
know he's got friends at Corpus Christi lookin' to help
him. Have him give Billboard a call at the cafe, okay?"

The redhead thought about it for several seconds,
staring into the space between Macky and Billboard. The
stocky kid with the glistening eyes continued to play the
knife blade across his pantleg, hopeful that he'd have
a chance to use it. Macky was checking the terrain out
of the corner of his eye, looking for quick cover or
something he could use as a shield when the action broke
out, when suddenly the confrontation ended. The
redhead turned abruptly and walked back down the alley.
After a moment's hesitation, the others followed without
a word. The little badass with the nervous blade was the
last to go, but he went.

Macky felt a shiver work its way down his arms to his
fingertips. He hoped Billboard didn't see the slight
tremor in his hands, but he needn't have worried.

"Man!" Billboard said softly, as the gangbangers
disappeared around a bend in the alley. "I ain't been that
scared since my first shower up at Arcadia."

# CHAPTER 9

$W$hile Billboard and Macky were chasing down a bus on Backus Avenue, Sergeants Hafner and Greene were in the southeast suburb of Densmore, caught in a traffic snarl. They had just completed a fruitless trip to the home of the late Alan Everett Muncy, the dead camper, to inform his wife of his death. Fruitless because the man's wife wasn't there.

"So she didn't go back to work after lunch," Greene said. "Didn't call in sick or anything—she just didn't show up back at her desk."

"And she isn't home, either," Hafner said. "Unless she's in bed with a wet wash towel over her eyes, a couple Seconals in her system, the blinds pulled."

"Yeah, but wouldn't she at least have called in if she got a migraine and had to take the afternoon off?"

"You'd think so." Hafner saw a small opening in the right lane and squeezed over. "Also, it's pretty coincidental that on the day her husband gets shot down in a midtown parking lot, she drops out of sight without a word."

"Which moves her to the head of the list for hubby's homicide."

"She's the whole list at this point."

"Well, we'll have to see what her co-workers have to say."

Hafner grunted. "If we get outa this bottleneck before the bank closes."

"You should've used the bubble." The bubble, as Greene called it, was the removable flashing light that could be popped onto the roof for emergency calls.

"It's not an emergency. Besides, how was I supposed to know we'd get caught in the middle of this? Whatever this is."

Greene let it go, both men slipping into silence for a couple of minutes as they waited for the traffic to move. Then Greene said, "I still say you owe me a lunch at Verelli's. You beeped me away from a slab of lasagna."

"The lieutenant owes you. I was just in the wrong place at the right time."

"Again. Which you wouldn't have been if you'd go out to lunch with the rest of us once in a while, 'stead of always brown bagging it at your desk."

"I don't always brown-bag—me and you eat at The Hard Time Cafe just about every Thursday. Besides, bringing your own lunch is sound fiscal practice." Hafner had been reading *Money* magazine of late, looking for ways to retire early and still buy that new RV he had his eye on. After all, what was the point of having a plush new camper if you didn't have the time to really put it to use? And vice versa. "You should try it sometime, save yourself a ton of money."

"Maybe if I had a wife at home to make it for me."

The comment took Hafner back to his wife, Marie, and the argument they'd had days before: he wanting to trade in their twelve-year-old recreational vehicle for something bigger and better, she saying they could put a built-in pool in the backyard for a third of the price and use the savings to go out to dinner once in a while.

He looked at his partner and said with Confucian gravity, "Careful what you wish for—you may get it."

"Speaking of which," Greene said, "did you say anything to Garafino about that Lorret County request on Sean Carpenter?"

"Like what? Like did I beg him to let me add it to our already overflowing caseload? So we can run around up on Backus Ave looking for one of Costello's yops?" Hafner's word for the kids in Corpus Christi's Youth Outreach Program. "No, I didn't do that."

"It's not like we're *that* backed up. And I *did* sort of promise Father Joe we'd keep a hand in."

"*You* promised Costello maybe, but I didn't."

What he *had* done, however, was explain the situation to the lieutenant and suggest he and Greene give the uniforms a little backup, if and when the opportunity arose. But he didn't want to tell that to Greene, who might think he was going soft for the priest and his collection of bad boys. So he said instead, "It's a department-wide BOL, right? So if we should happen to drive up to the north side on our way back to Metro, we're already under orders to be on the lookout for the kid. If we spot him, or learn something from one of his homies along the way, it's all in a day's work."

Greene was grinning over at him. "You're one of a kind, Harold."

"Yeah. Me and the Pope."

Their lane began to move suddenly, and Hafner was able to steer the unmarked Ford off onto a side street. Five minutes later they pulled in at the bank branch where Mrs. Muncy was employed. It was a typical suburban branch, squat and glassy, plopped down in the middle of a shopping strip's vast parking lot, the better for cars to snake their way past the drive-up ATMs.

Which made Greene think. "Jeez, when's the last time you can remember speaking face-to-face with a bank teller?"

"About two minutes from now," Hafner replied.

It turned out they didn't speak to any tellers but to a Mr. Morgensen, the branch manager. His office was small and neat and anonymous, decorated in various shades of oatmeal and quiet as an IRS waiting room. The full-length window behind his desk afforded a spiffy view of the Wager's supermarket that anchored the west end of the strip mall.

"As I said on the phone, gentlemen," Morgensen was saying, "Mrs. Muncy is normally a highly dependable woman. She's been a loan officer at this branch for, what, eight years?" He glanced at the woman seated beside his desk for confirmation. "And I don't think she's ever had an unscheduled absence. But Gloria here has worked directly with her all that time and I think it would be better for you to talk to her."

Gloria was in her mid-thirties, a little plump but well rounded, with heavily sprayed lemon-blond hair and crimson lip gloss. The lilac scent she was wearing carried to every corner of the office. Exactly the type of female Hafner was attracted to. Not that he'd ever, ever cheat on Marie, but a man could speculate, couldn't he? He let Greene take the lead on the questioning, the better to sit back and observe.

"So, Gloria," Greene said, calling up his most disarming smile, "do you know what time it was when Mrs. Muncy left work today?"

"Yes, it was about a quarter to twelve. She said she wanted to take an early lunch, that she had something she needed to do."

"Needed to do? She put it like that, did she?"

"Yes, exactly. I remember because she'd seemed distracted all morning. She'd given me several loan applications to process and I found a few that had errors—no signatures, that sort of thing—and that's not like Susan. She's usually very, very efficient." Gloria suddenly scissored her legs, uncrossing and then recrossing them in a way that better exposed the dimples on her knees and caused Hafner's heart to momentarily fibrillate.

Greene said, "Did she give you any indication of what was troubling her or what she needed to take care of?"

"No, we didn't really have time to chat at all this morning. Susan was rushing—I guess so she could clear her desk before taking off."

"Did she say anything to you about taking off the rest of the day?"

"No, in fact she said she'd be back by one-thirty. That's why I'm so surprised she hasn't come back. Something's happened to her, hasn't it? I mean, that's why you're here—"

Greene sat back. "We're here, ma'am, because right around noon today someone shot and killed Mrs. Muncy's husband downtown."

Gloria gasped, her hand automatically covering her mouth. Morgensen, having been informed earlier of the murder, merely sat there looking glum.

"Gloria," Greene said, "was Mrs. Muncy having any problems with Mr. Muncy that you're aware of?"

"No. Well, not really." She blinked, wide-eyed, at the two detectives. "I mean, they've been married a long time. Sure, she'd drop a remark once in a while."

"What sort of remarks?"

"Oh, you know, just general stuff. Saying men are all alike, little boys who play with great big toys, or complaining that she has to do ninety percent of the housework even though they both have full-time careers. I mean, it's nothing I haven't said about my own husband."

For the first time, Hafner noticed the wedding band on her finger and he was for some irrational reason disappointed. He said to her, "So there wasn't anything in particular that was bothering her?"

"I don't think—well—" She stuck a well-manicured red fingernail into her mouth and nipped at it, then dropped the hand back into her lap as is she'd been caught raiding the cookie jar. "There's the thing with the camper. I know that bothers her."

"You mean the Winnebago Muncy drove to work?" Hafner clarified.

"Yes, the big RV. Alan bought it last year sometime, I think, so they could camp on the weekends, but Susan never really got into it. She only did it to please Alan. I know for a fact she preferred a nice beach resort in Florida or trips to New York, but who wouldn't?"

Hafner said, "You'd be surprised."

Greene asked Gloria if she thought it was an emotional issue for Mrs. Muncy—enough to push her to take drastic actions.

"Oh, no! My God, no. I mean, that's crazy to think Susan would shoot her husband over the family camper."

She looked to Morgensen, who nodded weakly, still half-thinking of how he might shuffle the staff. "Or shoot anyone. It's, well, it's almost laughable—"

"Does she own a gun?"

Hafner's aggressive tone, as much as the question itself, brought Gloria back to earth.

"Um, well, yes, as a matter of fact, she does. For protection. I've seen it in her purse before." She added, "It's really small."

Hafner said, "So was the hole in Muncy's chest."

# CHAPTER 10

On Friday evening at 6:50,
with forty minutes until the final prayers of the day, a
weary Father Costello was in the abbot's office, waiting
for a phone call. Through the window he could see part
of the redwood-and-stone wing of the building that
housed the chapel. Beyond that was a sliver of wooded
hillside and a path that led eventually to the grotto.

Despite everything that had happened in the last two
days, a kind of nostalgia came over him. The feeling had
begun when he approached the monastery grounds out
along Valley Road two hours earlier. For a mile he saw no
buildings, just rolling fields of wheat and corn, orchards
and vegetable gardens separated by windbreaks of tall
trees. Here and there, a monk in green work clothes and
a broad-brimmed straw hat would appear, hunched over
a row of peas or an explosion of squash vines.

As he guided his little red Honda Civic up the gravel
drive to the abbey, he took in the buildings. There were

the modern yet rustic T-shaped main building and the barns and storage sheds downslope. The long, narrow bakery was in back, fronted by a separate driveway for the trucks that brought in supplies and hauled away thousands of loaves of Thy Daily Bread each week. With a little imagination, he could see the monastery as a medieval place, an enclave of civilization and morality in the tenth-century forests of Europe. A place of tradition, commerce, hope, and salvation.

The phone on the desk rang.

"Father Joe? Can you hear me all right?" Sister Matthew's voice came through clearly, if with a bit of metallic echo. "Oh, good. We have the speaker phone on, here in your office. Reuben and William and Chester are with me, as you requested."

"Good. I wanted to bring everyone up to speed on what's going on here at the abbey, and what I've learned from talking with people this afternoon. Also, Billboard, I wanted to hear if you had any luck up on Backus Avenue."

"Hard to say, Father. We might get a call, we might not." He described the episode with the gangbangers from the Back Boys, leaving out the intimidation with the knives. "If Sean's being hid out by that crew, he at least oughta hear we're looking for him and ready to help him, whatever the deal."

"Yes, that's good." *Whatever* the deal. The phrase resonated for Father Joe. Was he truly ready to help Sean Carpenter, no matter what? If, God forbid, the boy had murdered Brother John?

It was a question he'd been wrestling with since first hearing of the tragedy. There should have been no question. As a priest, he was in the forgiveness business, God's middleman. It was his job to help sinners renounce their sins and return to the grace of the Almighty. He had

heard the confessions of child abusers and wife beaters;
he had counseled murderers and rapists and every other
form of human predator.

And in every case he had been able to make the sign
of the cross over them and murmur the words of
absolution. Send them on their way with hope, at least,
for their salvation. But he never before had felt a
personal responsibility for another person's actions, as
if he were an accessory to the crime.

Could he really help Sean—forgive Sean—without
doing a disservice to the memory of his old friend and
mentor, Brother John Kolumus?

It had been twenty-two years now since he'd first met
the strong, outgoing Trappist. As a seminarian about to
become ordained, Joseph Costello was required to
complete a three-month retreat as part of his final
training. He had been assigned to the Abbey of the
Ganannoqua and to Brother John personally. It was
wintertime, and he was young and energetic and
idealistic. Too much so, perhaps, to take easily to the
uneventful but strict life inside a monastery.

It was with a rueful smile he recalled his first full day
at the abbey. Awakened at 2:00 A.M.; calisthenics on the
cold floor of his room. The stiff walk through the January
snow to vigils in the chapel. He still remembered those
first spoken words of the day, uttered every morning by
the communicant, "O Lord, open my lips," and the group
response, "And my mouth shall declare your praise." Then
the spartan breakfast of black coffee and dry bread and
cranberry juice, followed by a three-hour work shift.

And the raisins! Dear Lord, never let him forget the
raisins.

That had been his job assignment that first morning
and many mornings thereafter. To load box after heavy

box of raisins onto a screen, then crush and stack the empty boxes as the raisins were run through the raisin washing machine. Meanwhile, he and old Brother Carlo were careful to listen for any telltale ping or scrape that revealed the presence of a pebble or a twig or even a stray bit of cardboard. It was a tedious, mindless, exhausting job. Not as noisy as oiling the hundreds of bread pans, or as wickedly warm as working the hot bread line at the ovens. Or as finger-numbing as slipping loaf after loaf of freshly sliced bread into its bag and stacking it, all of which he would also do many times in his three months at the abbey.

But washing raisins would always be the most memorable image for Father Joe, because it was his introduction to the humble life of the Trappist monk. And because he would never forget Brother John's words to him, upon finding him half asleep that day in the dining room for the midday meal. He began with a quotation from St. Benedict of Nursia, the patriarch of Christian monasticism.

"'When they live by the labor of their hands, as our fathers and the apostles did, then they are truly monks,'" Brother John recited sternly. Then he grinned and clapped a big, callused hand across the young seminarian's back. "Think of us as the Marine Corps of the clergy, Joseph, and this as your basic training. Everything that comes after should be like a walk in the park."

He could feel that clap on the back now as he sat behind the abbot's desk, gazing out the window. Brother John, that stern bear of a monk with a soft streak as wide as his smile—he would miss him dearly. And it would be difficult, perhaps impossible, to forgive his killer, no matter what Father Joe's vows and vocation were.

But he was allowing pessimism to cloud his judgment.

As deeply as he felt Brother John's loss, he believed in Sean Carpenter's innocence. There had to be some other explanation . . .

"Hey, Father, you still there?"

"What?" Father Joe shook off his reverie and held the phone tighter to his ear. "Yes, yes. I'm still here, Billboard."

"So, uh, you went out yourself today and did a little digging?"

"A bit, yes." He told them about his visit with Mrs. Witoviak, from whom he learned that two of the Backus Avenue Boys had been down to Garfield recently, looking for Sean. He also described his talk with Mike Keller, who said Marco Pilato was one of the gang members who had come down and that Sean was upset by the visit.

"Apparently he was of two minds," Father Joe said. "In some ways he missed the camaraderie of the gang, but at the same time he feared and resented its influence on his life. It's possible that this conflict convinced him to just take off." He related the fantasy shared by Sean and Mike Keller, to take off cross-country and drive to California.

But the others weren't as ready to accept this option.

"That would be some coincidence, Father," said the voice of Chet Tomzak, the cafe's business manager. "The day Brother John is killed, Sean decides to hitch a ride west? Even if he did head for California, it has to be connected."

Billboard argued, "Just because the kid flew doesn't mean he did the deed, man. Maybe he saw it happen and ran off scared, or maybe he knew something about— about I don't know what. Hey, Father, did you find out anything like that?"

Father Joe thought back to what Mike Keller had said: how Sean, after being reprimanded for looking at pornography on the Internet, had claimed to have

something on Brother John. Father Joe couldn't imagine
what it could be, other than the boasting of a young man
whose ego had been injured. "No," he told Billboard.
"Nothing relevant."

They passed a few more minutes talking, with Sister
Matty promising to call the sergeants and ask them once
again to use their influence in locating Sean. Billboard
volunteered to return to the Backus Avenue
neighborhood to do some more searching, and Reuben
Macky reluctantly agreed to go along. Chet would hold
down the fort at the cafe.

After ringing off, Father Joe sat in the swivel chair,
looking blindly out the window and thinking. That was
how the abbot found him when he came into the office.
He began to get up, but Father Mazewski waved him
down again.

"It never fails, you know," the abbot said with a smile.
"Everyone who visits us for any length of time soon finds
the telephone. It's a lifeline to the outside world, I
suppose, reassuring to know that you haven't quite
dropped off the face of the earth."

"There are times when I wish I could." Father Joe
sighed. "Father, what happened? I know that's the
question of the hour, but I don't know what else to do
but ask it of you."

"Unfortunately, I can't answer it. I have no idea why
Sean, or anyone else, would want to do harm to
Brother John."

"Is there anything, any simmering rivalries or—I don't
know—any feuds between the brothers?" He knew he
was grasping for straws in the wind, but there was
nothing else he could do.

The abbot slowly shook his head. "The truth, Joe? In
this self-contained place of ours, a small tiff is felt more

deeply than any world-shaking event outside, and the results often are more disastrous." As Father Joe opened his mouth to react, the abbot held up a hand to stop him. "But—and this is the all-important but—despite the daily potential for misunderstandings to build up, I honestly don't believe there is anyone inside this abbey capable of the sort of violence that killed Brother John. And I say that not as an abbot protecting his flock, Joe, but as a former prosecuting attorney."

"Someone from outside, then? A drifter, looking for a handout, perhaps stumbles across Brother John meditating in the grotto and—"

"And stabs him because Brother John refused to help him? How likely would that be, Joe, that John would refuse a poor man?"

"I know, Father Paul, it's ridiculous. I'm just—tired, I suppose."

"Well, we'll be better able to speculate in the morning," the abbot said. "The autopsy report is due tomorrow, according to Sergeant Podesta, and that may tell us something useful, although I can't imagine what." He gestured to the phone. "Did you reach the sergeant, by the way?"

"No, he was off-duty and they wouldn't give me his home phone number."

"Mm. I know you're eager to speak to him, but that can wait until tomorrow too. He'll be around the grounds, I'm sure, if only to hound poor Brother Jerome for the answers to his list of questions. In the meantime, can I suggest we walk to the chapel together? Compline is in another fifteen minutes."

\*     \*     \*

A short time later, Father Joe Costello sat in a pew amongst the monks of the Abbey of the Ganannoqua, singing in low, sonorous voices the psalms in praise of the Lord. He began to feel a little better in tune with his world and his God. It was as if that huge granite slab that formed the altar had been laying across his heart and Father Mazewski, as he stood before it with hands and voice upraised, had lifted it, relieving Father Joe of its weight.

Faith renewed was hope renewed, he reminded himself as he sang. In the silent moment that followed, he said a prayer for Brother John and another for Sean.

In closing, Father Paul Mazewski, his words echoing from the exposed roof rafters, intoned, "May the almighty and merciful Lord grant us a restful night."

To which Father Joe Costello and all the monks responded: "And a peaceful death."

# CHAPTER 11

Brother Malthius stumbled, nearly spilling the tray of loaves he was carrying to the cooling racks. They were whole wheat, which, while not as heavy as the raisin bread loaves, still always seemed heavier to him than the white loaves. Or perhaps it was merely that the whole wheat came second, after a run of white, which meant he was more fatigued. On the other hand . . .

"Brother Malthius?"

The spoken words jarred him as surely as if he'd been bumped and, once again, the tray began to tip. He managed to slide it onto the rack in one deft motion, however, and turned toward the voice that had broken the silence of the bakery with his name. It was the parish priest from Corpus Christi, Father Costello, smiling kindly through that trim red beard of his. Brother Malthius returned the smile and raised one eyebrow as if to ask, *What is it I can do for you, Father?*

"I'm sorry," the priest said, keeping his voice as low as possible considering the whir of the machines. "But I don't remember enough sign to observe the customary silence in here. Could we go somewhere to talk for a few minutes, Brother?"

Malthius glanced across the room. Brother Gabriel, the head baker, was busy overseeing the blending of the raisins into the dough in the three huge stainless steel mixer bowls. Malthius nodded to Father Costello, grateful for the interruption and the temporary relief from the heat and noise. He led him up the three steps from the bakery floor and down a short corridor to the office.

"How may I help you, Father Costello," Brother Malthius asked, taking one of the small office's two chairs.

Father Joe took the other, beside the room's only window. He looked out for a moment, watching the morning sun spread across the sloping bean fields as he composed his thoughts. He had risen in the pre-dawn darkness to attend vigils with the monks at 3:30 A.M. and lauds two hours later. In between the psalm singing there had been a simple breakfast of toast and juice and coffee and, for Father Costello, an hour of contemplation in the library. But he had found no answers there, only more questions.

Now, as the clock on the office wall moved toward 7:30, he turned to the youthful Brother Malthius and asked the first thing that came into his head. "I understand you found Brother John out on the grotto path. I wonder if you could tell me about it."

"Tell you about it, Father?"

"What you saw, what impressions you have of that moment. Anything that stands out in your mind." His shoulders heaved. "I know I'm being vague, Brother. Grasping for straws, I believe, is the apt phrase. I suppose

I'm hoping you'll recall something that can make some sense of this for me."

Brother Malthius shook his head slowly. "I'm sorry, but I doubt I can help you any more than I've been able to help myself. None of it makes any sense to my scattered mind, I'm afraid. It's too much to take in, really, that John is actually dead, that Sean could've done something like this—"

"We don't know that he did," Father Joe interrupted gently. "But what makes you think it was Sean, Brother Malthius?"

"Well, I—" It was the timid monk's turn to shrug. "Sean's gone, isn't he? That has to mean something."

"Something, yes, but not necessarily that he killed Brother John."

"Well, if not Sean, then one of his friends. Those boys from the gang—"

"The Backus Avenue Boys?"

"Yes, with the red jackets. Two of them came to see Sean not long ago. Maybe they hatched some kind of plot against Brother John, a robbery or something."

"Hmm." Father Joe stroked his bearded chin. "I knew they were looking for Sean, but I didn't know they were bold enough to show up at the abbey."

"Oh, no, Father, they didn't actually come onto the grounds. I was working in the cherry orchard one afternoon—I suppose it was maybe ten days ago now. Anyway, I saw a car parked down along the river road, a large, older car. Then Sean left the grounds on his bike, heading for home, and he stopped to talk with the two young men in the car. They spoke for several minutes. I told this to Father Mazewski and Sergeant Podesta already, by the way."

"As you should have. Still, it's a stretch, isn't it? To assume the Back Boys would come back days later and attack Brother John. For what reason?"

"I don't know, Father, but then none of it makes any sense." Malthius leaned forward, his slim fingers draped over his knees. "You know, it could've been something as simple as an argument that got out of hand. They used to fight, you know. Argue, I mean. Sean had quite a temper."

"Mm, as did Brother John, if I remember correctly. But I still couldn't imagine *him* killing someone."

"Well, no. But I don't think it's quite the same thing. Brother John was a mature person, in control of himself, even if he did lose his patience now and then. But Sean— Sean was undisciplined and immature, not to mention profane." Malthius colored slightly and pointed at the computer that occupied its own corner desk. "You've heard about the sort of material Sean was viewing on that thing? Pornogaphy," he added in a near whisper.

"Yes, I did hear about that." Father Joe was a parish priest who heard confessions weekly, as well as a counselor to ex-cons and delinquent youths. He was much harder to shock than a simple monk who spent his life hidden within the insular world of the monastery. "But let's get back to my original question for now, Brother. Think about your immediate thoughts and reactions when you found John's body. Other than grief and shock, of course, was there anything else that stands out in your mind?"

The monk gnawed at his lower lip as he considered the question. "Well, yes, there was the irony, I'd guess you'd call it, of Brother John dying in the grotto. He considered the Stations of the Cross, all those life-sized wood carvings, something for the tourists. If not a sacrilege, then in bad taste. It was one of the few things he and Brother Chan agreed on. Neither one of them ever walks the grotto path."

"Interesting," Father Joe murmured. He glanced out the window again. "So what you're suggesting is that, since Brother John never walked there on his own, this must've been an arranged meeting of some kind. He was lured to the grotto—"

But Brother Malthius was waving his hands in protest. "Please, Father Costello, I made no such suggestion. I merely said John didn't like to walk the grotto path. Your imagination filled in the rest."

Just then, Walter Monday walked into the office, briefcase in hand. He stopped short at the sight of the priest and the monk, his broad, fleshy face suddenly flashing a darker shade of pink. "Oh, excuse me. I didn't realize anyone was in here. I'll, um, wait outside—"

"It's all right; we're about done here anyway." Father Joe said. He stood and introduced himself, shaking the big man's limp hand.

"It's a pleasure to meet you, Father. I mean—" Monday grew pinker still. "—not under these circumstances, certainly."

Brother Malthius stepped in. "Mr. Monday is with Wager's, the supermarket chain. They buy all our bread for their stores."

"Yes," Father Joe nodded. "I shop there myself." Or at least, Mrs. Clooney, the rectory's housekeeper, did. And she was always sure to bring home a loaf or two of Thy Daily Bread. He smiled to put the big man at ease. "You're up and about bright and early on a Saturday morning, Mr. Monday. Is that the Trappist influence rubbing off on you?"

"In the bakery business we're all early risers, Father. Freshness is the watchword, which means early-morning bakes and constant shipments and—well, listen to me go on. I'm sure you're not interested in all that. The fact is, while I do try to come by at least once a week to see how the bake is going, I don't ordinarily come on Saturday. But, given the circumstances, the emotions running so high around here, and with John gone, I thought I might be needed to get the shipping orders sorted out if for nothing else." Monday heaved a sigh and set his briefcase on the desk beside the computer. "You're down for the special memorial Mass this evening for Brother John, I take it?"

"Yes." Among other things.

"I'll be coming back myself later for the Mass. He was quite a man. We've done business together for almost sixteen years. I guess I never even realized, until he was gone, just how close I felt—" He broke off and turned away, fiddling with the clasps on his briefcase.

"He'll be greatly missed by all of us," Father Joe said.

"Indeed, he will," said Malthius. "Well, Father Costello, if you're through with me, I'd better get back to work. St. Benedict is looking down on us, after all."

"Yes, he is. Thanks for your time, Brother."

As Malthius left the office, Walter Monday turned around again, the moistness in his eyes the only hint of his emotions. "I didn't mean to drive you out, Father. I only need the computer for a half hour or so, and then you're welcome to use the office for—whatever."

Father Joe decided to come clean. He told him of his relationship with Sean Carpenter, as well as his ties to Brother John.

Monday tilted his head quizzically. "And so you're investigating on your own?"

"Well, no. Looking for some answers, certainly. I guess you could say I'm trying to make some sense of things, for my own peace of mind."

"Some things don't make sense, Father. They just are." His fleshy face sagged into a basset hound's frown. "My own wife, Vera, passed on six years ago from cancer. A sweeter person you've never met. But that's life, isn't it? Sometimes the good die young."

"I'm sorry for your loss," Father Joe said solemnly. "Still, I like to think there's some greater purpose behind things, Mr. Monday—"

"Please, call me Walt. I didn't mean to sidetrack the conversation. It's just, one sad death makes a person think back to others."

Father Joe nodded. "And I didn't mean to open a theological discussion, Walt. But I would like to ask you a few questions if you could spare me a few minutes."

"Well." The big man glanced at the briefcase next to the computer, then at his watch. "Certainly, uh, Father Costello. I have some paperwork to record, but that can wait."

"Good. And call me Joe." Father Joe waited for Monday to settle himself onto the desk chair. He remained standing himself, leaning back against the edge of the office's credenza. "As the abbey's business contact, you and Brother John worked closely together?"

"Oh, yes, as I said. Actually, the stuff I plan to do in here today isn't part of my job; it was John's job. But I know what he would've done, bookkeeping-wise, to get today's bake sent out; I've certainly seen him do it enough times. So I decided I'd better pinch-hit until Father Mazewski and the men appoint a replacement." Monday's eyes widened. "Gosh, I hadn't thought about that before. I have no idea who they'll appoint as their new business manager. I don't think any of the other brothers have any business background."

"Surely one of them can learn. They're well-educated men. Brother John didn't have any business background, either, as I recall."

"That's true, he was an educator before he joined the order," Monday said. "But there's a huge difference. He took over management of the bakery some twenty-odd years ago, when the monks were baking a few hundred extra loaves for sale in the abbey gift shop and down at the Garfield IGA. He was able to grow into the job as the bakery itself grew. But now—" He threw up his hands. "—we're talking an annual gross of nearly two-and-a-half million dollars, Father."

"I had no idea."

"It's no mom-and-pop operation anymore. I mean, yes, the fundamentals are still the same. But we're talking relatively large numbers on a weekly basis. Suppliers that have to be paid, supplies ordered, truck transport— although, since Wager's has an exclusive for all the abbey's output, we arrange all the shipping via our company trucks."

"I should have realized, this is big business."

"Well, yes and no, Father. That two-point-five million dollar figure is the gross, remember. The abbey's profit per loaf, after subtracting production costs, is about thirty-five cents. So annual profits come in under a million dollars. And it's a nonprofit situation, this being a religious institution, which means the money isn't treated as taxable income. And that's only fair," he added, "seeing that what they don't spend to support themselves, they put out into various charitable programs."

Father Joe knew all about nonprofits and religious charities, thanks to his work at Corpus Christi. He knew, for example, that while nonprofits didn't have to pay income taxes on their earnings, they did have to justify themselves to the IRS each year with a slew of paperwork. Which brought to mind another question.

"How *was* Brother John able to keep up with the accounting for an enterprise this size? Before they went to computers, I mean."

"Well, for years he did it the old-fashioned way, with a ledger book and double-entry bookkeeping. He used a quill pen, in fact." Monday smiled at the gaping priest. "Only kidding, Father. About the quill pen, I mean. That was an old joke between John and me. As for the ledger, it wasn't as bad as it sounds because of the abbey bakery being an exclusive supplier for Wager's. Since we're their only customer, we allow the abbey to work off our records, supplying John with monthly statements on gross shipments, unit costs, unsold product, even percentage breakdowns on what sold best in a given week—the whole wheat, the white, or the raisin bread. Getting the computer was just a way for John to organize the material better and faster and allow Wager's to send over our statements electronically."

"Then, I'm not sure I understand why Sean Carpenter was needed—"

"Oh. Well, as I understand it, Sean's role was important in helping the abbey get more out of the computer's potential, like creating a Web site. John learned the basics for doing the bakery bookkeeping, how to use the spreadsheet and financial software, but that was about it. Frankly, I'm the same way. The company supplies me with a laptop and I know how to use it to do the basic things I need to do—placing and routing orders from my bread suppliers—but don't ask me how to download the latest computer game from the Internet. I'd be lost."

"Yes, the Internet." Father Joe pronounced the word with the slight skepticism accorded it by the uninitiated and the computer-challenged, of which he was both. "I've heard, Walt, that Sean had gotten himself into some trouble regarding his choice of subject matter that he was accessing."

"You mean the, uh, porno stuff." Monday was clearly uncomfortable talking of such things with a priest. "And then there was the Satanism too, but I really think that was just more boyish experimentation. After all, Sean's just a teenage boy—"

"I hadn't been told about that. Satanism?"

Monday shrugged. "That's what John told me. I guess there are Web sites for just about everything under the sun these days. Or the full moon. Anyway, John was very upset about it."

"This came after Brother John had already reprimanded Sean for accessing pornographic materials?" When Monday nodded, Father Joe pressed on, frowning. "What were the circumstances, do you know? I mean, did he catch him red-handed or—?"

"I understand that John, after the first run-in over the porn stuff, had a way of checking on which sites Sean accessed. Some kind of electronic log or something that's kept by the Internet provider, I think." Monday pinked up again. "I'm sorry, Father Joe, but like I said, I'm not really up on these things."

"Oh, no, you've been very helpful. I appreciate your time."

"Not at all." He reached into the pocket of his suitcoat and extracted a card. "If I can be of any further help, Father, here's my home phone, as well as Wager's business office in Riverton and my cell phone."

"Thank you, Walt. I, uh, suppose I'll see you later at the memorial Mass."

"Yes. Something I'm not looking forward to, I'm afraid. But I wouldn't miss it." Monday sighed, then turned away, again busying himself with his briefcase.

# CHAPTER 12

The grotto was cool and still, shaded by the ash, oak, maple, and birch trees that dotted the rocky hillocks. It was mid-morning and Father Joe, like his hosts, had been up for nearly seven hours already. Unlike the monks, however, he hadn't spent his time toiling in the bakery and the fields and the laundry. Instead, he had made his rounds, speaking to anyone and everyone about Brother John and Sean Carpenter, looking for answers, for reason in an unreasonable world. Finding nothing and trying to keep himself from Walter Monday's brand of fatalism: *Some things don't make sense, Father. They just are.*

He couldn't accept that. He *wouldn't* accept it. Somewhere there were answers to this tragedy. Perhaps even inside his own head if only he were intelligent enough—brave enough—to examine everything he'd learned, pick out the important pieces, and form them into the proper picture.

*The Backus Avenue Boys, the abbey's computer, the pornographic Web sites, Satanism, Brother John's aversion for the grotto, Brother Chan's disapproval of the bread business. Sean caught in the middle of all that. Brother John stabbed to death in the small hours of the morning. Sean suddenly gone missing. Missing and presumed hiding out back up in the Backus Avenue neighborhood or thumbing his way to golden California. Or possibly, if Sean were innocent, missing and presumed . . .*

"No!" Father Joe muttered the word forcefully. And yet, even in his denial, he recognized that he was merely avoiding a thought that had wormed its way into his brain almost from the beginning. A thought so painful, he had submerged it as deeply as he could. But it was a thought that would not stay hidden; he had to have the courage to think it and then to examine it.

*All right, then.*

He was seated on a crude wooden bench, fashioned from a section of tree trunk that had been sawed lengthwise, then sanded smooth on top and left to weather naturally alongside the grotto path. Leaning forward slightly, he placed his palms flat on either side of him and took a deep breath. And thought the thought.

*If Sean were innocent and missing, it didn't naturally have to follow that he, too, had fallen victim to whoever had murdered Brother John. But it had to be considered. Dear Lord, it had to be considered.*

"Excuse me, uh, Father Costello?"

"Yes?" Father Joe jerked his head up. The man standing a few feet away on the rough wood chips of the grotto path was of medium height and stocky, square of jaw, with dark hair that was receding into a widow's peak. He wore a lightweight blue sport coat and baggy gray slacks and a striped tie with a loosened knot. Father Joe had encountered enough police officers over the years to know one when he saw one.

"You must be Sergeant Podesta." He began to rise from the bench but was waved back in place by the other man.

"It's still too early in the day for formalities if you ask me." Podesta was carrying a mug of steaming coffee, one of the large china mugs from the dining hall. His hands were wrapped around it with the reverence a priest reserves for the communion chalice.

He took a sip and sighed. "That's one thing they don't skimp on, the coffee. Best cup I've had in a coon's age."

Father Joe smiled, thinking back to his days at the abbey, when the morning mug of strong black coffee was like ambrosia. "Yes, it's about the only stimulant they allow themselves," he said. "Well, perhaps the occasional glass of hard cider or sacramental wine."

"I don't suppose I'll ever understand this life here, despite Father Mazewski's attempts to educate me." Podesta sipped again and shook his head minutely. "The solitude would kill me after a while. All these somber faces, day after day of the same joyless routine—"

"Oh, no, not joyless, Sergeant. Remember, you're seeing the brothers under adverse circumstances, to put it mildly. But in better times I think you'd see a kind of serenity in these men that you might find enviable. They live the way they do, after all, because they sincerely believe it brings them closer to God."

"Well, maybe so." The whole religion thing struck him as a kind of wishful thinking, like a twelve-year-old who steadfastly holds onto a belief in Santa Claus. "I, uh, understand you've been trying to reach me, Father."

"Yes, to ask you where your investigation stands. And, if I'm not being too presumptuous, to share information on the case."

"Uh-huh." Podesta rested one foot on the end of the bench. "First thing you need to realize, Father, is that this is a murder investigation. If you have any pertinent information, it's your legal obligation to come forward."

"Of course. I wasn't suggesting a quid pro quo or anything, Sergeant. I only hoped you'd hear me out, and perhaps we could examine together some of the possibilities—"

"Suppose you tell me what you've come up with. We'll play the rest by ear."

"Certainly." Father Joe told him what Malthius had said about Brother John disliking the depictions of the Stations of the Cross and thus avoiding the grotto path. "It has to make you wonder, doesn't it? Why would John be down here first thing in the morning if he had an aversion for the place?"

"Huh." Podesta thought about it, slowly shaking his head. Thought about the priest too, and how much he wanted to tell him. Decided it could be useful, sharing information with an insider. *Some* information, anyway. But first, some ground rules. He said, "This is between you and me, understand, Father? I don't want anyone else at this monastery to know what I'm about to tell you. Not yet, anyway."

"I understand, Sergeant."

"What you've just told me could fit in with one of the medical examiner's findings. Or I should say speculations." He looked dourly into the other man's eyes. "It's likely the body was moved."

"Moved? From where?"

"Don't know that. In fact, we don't even know for sure that it was moved. The M.E. only says that the lividity— that's basically where the blood pools inside the body in the first hours after death—*suggests* the body may've been moved. If it happened at all, it happened less than an hour after death occurred. Too soon for lividity to have been completed, which is why the M.E. can't tell for sure."

Father Joe was nodding as he eagerly listened to the sergeant's words. "You know what this means, don't you? If the body was moved, Sean Carpenter couldn't have been the killer. He's five-seven, a hundred-forty pounds. Brother John was a strapping six-footer. And dead weight is even harder to move—"

But Podesta stopped him, holding up a finger. "First, Father, we don't know for sure that the body was moved, although it looks likely. Second, it doesn't mean the Carpenter kid didn't do the murder; it only means he had help. Like maybe one or more of his pals from that gang he belonged to. Word is they'd been down to see him recently, trying to get him back in the fold. It's possible Brother John tried to intervene and got killed for his trouble."

Father Joe opened his mouth to argue but quickly snapped it shut. The sergeant's scenario was as good as any other explanation, on the surface. He couldn't refute it.

"Anyway," Podesta continued, "between the postmortem findings and what you found out from Brother Malthius, we've inched the investigation forward some. For one thing, it means the murder didn't necessarily grow out of a prearranged meeting out in the woods, which is how I was looking at it from the beginning. He could've been killed anywhere, although probably it was in or near the bakery or the dining hall—"

"Why do you say that?"

"Something else in the M.E.'s report, only this time it isn't speculation. The victim was stabbed with a long, thick-bladed knife with a serrated edge. Almost certainly one of the big bread knives they use around here. The only places they keep those is the bakery and the little kitchen off the dining hall. One of my guys has taken a bread knife back to the medical examiner's office, so we'll soon have confirmation on that. Meanwhile, I've just sent crews into the bakery complex and the dining area to look for blood traces."

Father Joe could sit no more, such was the mental energy coursing through him. He stood and walked a few feet down the path, then back again to face Podesta. He was wearing what he thought of as "the uniform," his clerical collar and a black linen suit. The face beneath the neat red beard was solemn, the blue eyes doleful. *Just the way a priest is supposed to look*, thought the policeman.

"Sergeant, I know you're still looking at Sean as the perpetrator of this crime, and I know you have good reason," he said quietly. "But I'd ask you to look at the case from a different perspective, with Sean as a victim, just as Brother John was a victim."

Podesta held the priest's stare for a moment, then cleared his throat. "Are you suggesting, Father, that Sean Carpenter is dead?"

Thinking the words had been bad enough. Hearing them made Father Joe blanch.

"I think it's a very real possibility," he said. "No word of him has turned up back in his old neighborhood, amongst his old gang. Has your out-of-state alert turned up anything?"

"No. But it's been only twenty-four hours. A kid could hide out under a bridge for that long and not be spotted. You'll need more than that, Father, to convince me."

Father Joe didn't have more than that. Yet. But he believed the information was there, in his head, waiting to be deciphered.

Podesta, however, wasn't waiting any longer. "Anyway, it's been interesting, Father." He took a final swallow of the coffee and flipped the dregs out onto the ivy that formed a ground cover over most of the grotto. "I'll be around if you come up with anything solid for me. Meantime, I've got an investigation to run."

*     *     *

Brother Jerome wasn't any more receptive than he'd been in the abbot's office. This time they met at the hermit monk's hovel in the woods—Brother Jerome, Sergeant Podesta, and, as interpreter and referee, Father Mazewski. *Hovel* was the best word Podesta could come up with to describe the wizened little man's home. It was two parts dirt and sod, one part tar-paper shack; essentially, a wall of boards, a door, and a small window embedded into the side of a hill. Approaching it from the path farther up the hill, you'd never know it was there at all except for the piece of stovepipe that came up out of the ground.

Podesta had to admit, though, the view was pretty nice if you liked that sort of thing. The former root cellar looked down across a gentle slope crowded with paper birch trees and, farther on, a broad green pond. It was the same pond that curved around by the grotto, Mary's Pond. He wondered if there were any fish in it. Then he wondered it he shouldn't get a scuba team down there to search for the missing murder weapon, or even—

"Sergeant? Brother Jerome is speaking to you."

Podesta looked at the abbot, then at Brother Jerome, who was seated on a stump outside his hovel, looking in his coarse brown smock and matted beard like something out of a Tolkien fantasy. He was making some motions with his hands, directed at Podesta.

"Yeah, uh, three something. He's saying something about writing, and something about the number three, right?"

"Page three of his written deposition," Father Mazewski explained in that calm, cultured tone that

Podesta was beginning to find maddening. "He wants you to review what he's written on page three before you go."

"What, here? He wants me to read it here?"

"If you would. It must be something he thinks will need some interpretation."

The hermit monk had the informal deposition in his lap, several legal-sized yellow pages held together by a dog-eared corner. He offered it up with a hand that looked like the roots of an iron tree.

"Okay." Podesta found a fallen log nearby and sat, thumbing his way to page three. The writing was small and crabbed but readable. At least the words were. What the words added up to was a different story. The creases in the policeman's brow grew deeper the more he read.

"What is this? 'Under the shadows of the half moon and the eyes of God, a great bear descended on these woods and drank and gamboled in the pond.'" He looked up at the abbot. "He saw a bear out in the woods one night?"

It wasn't out of the question. Black bears had been seen only a score of miles to the south in recent years on state forest land. But Father Mazewski thought there might be another explanation.

"Brother Jerome is a bit of a mystic," he said, smiling down kindly at the hermit monk. "He may be writing metaphorically. Perhaps the bear represents danger or turmoil—"

But the old man shook his bald head firmly, and his hands fluttered into sign.

"No, he says it was a real bear, or something bearlike, that he saw," the abbot said. "In early morning, the day Brother John was killed. Early morning for Jerome—that would mean sometime before rising at 2:00 A.M. Yes. He says he was disturbed by something, couldn't sleep, and so he was out on his stump, listening to the woods."

Podesta was still reading, still frowning. "'Five rocks are missing from the grotto.' What's he mean—five specific rocks? Missing from where? There's rocks all over the place out here."

"Let me see." The abbot read over Podesta's shoulder. "Well, yes, it does say five rocks are missing." He turned back to Brother Jerome and exchanged a flurry of signs. "Hmm. Yes, he claims five large rocks, about the size of cantaloupes, are missing from various places in the woods."

"Just normal rocks?"

"It would seem so."

"From different places?"

Father Mazewski exchanged more sign with the hermit monk. "Yes, different places, but all down near the grotto stations, between the stations and the pond."

Podesta shook his head. Not for the first time in his career, he wondered why he hadn't become a fireman instead of a cop. "I'm supposed to believe he can tell that five random rocks have gone missing from these woods?"

"It's what he does, Sergeant," the abbot insisted. "Remember when I explained *lectio divina* to you? The divine reading? Well, Brother Jerome has been studying these woods for fifty years as his *lectio*. He knows every square inch of this place the way you or I know the contents of our offices. If he says five rocks are missing, they indeed are missing."

# CHAPTER
# 13

Sergeants Hafner and Greene turned up at The Hard Time Cafe late Saturday morning, in time to join in the general coffee break that always preceded the restaurant's opening for the lunch trade. Seated with them at a large round table in the middle of the dining room were Reuben Macky, Chet Tomzak, and Sister Matthew. All but the little nun had heavy china mugs of strong coffee. Matty had a small pot of orange pekoe tea.

"Nada. Zilch, zero, zip," Hafner was saying, leaning lazily back in his chair but careful to keep one hand in contact with his coffee, like a man who'd had too much Friday night. "Every place we checked up on Backus Avenue, we got the same answer. Nobody's seen Sean Carpenter in the 'hood, nobody's heard nothin', nobody knows nothin'."

"That could be the intimidation factor at work," Matty offered. "The Back Boys have a reputation for that sort of thing."

"True," Greene acknowledged. "It could be that's what's happening. Maybe they've got the Carpenter kid stashed someplace, protecting him. Maybe they got him wired up to a computer, working out some scam for Marco Pilato."

Chet Tomzak, who was watching their faces, said, "But you guys don't really think so."

Greene looked to his partner, who merely shrugged. "No," Greene said. "If we had to lay a bet, we'd say the kid's not up there."

"This is based on what?" Matty asked. "Just a feeling?"

"Basically, yes. Call it cop instinct if you like. We hear people lie to us every day, Sister. It gets so you can recognize bull—" He caught himself in time to clip the word off short. "—when you hear it. In this case, every informant, every friendly or community leader we talked to gave us the same answer. Marco and company have been swaggering around about as much as usual, no more, no less. And nobody's seen or heard mention of Sean Carpenter coming back."

"No disrespect intended," said Macky, his voice a low rumble. "But ain't that the idea, from the Back Boys' standpoint, I mean? Keep the kid under wraps. They coulda snuck him into some condemned tenement or the back of a crack house in the middle of the night, with nobody the wiser."

"Except for the Boys themselves," Hafner said. He leaned forward and wrapped both hands around the mug as if he could absorb the caffeine by osmosis. "Keeping secrets ain't their strong suit. If they had the kid holed up for a few days, with cops and you guys coming around looking for him, with the kid a suspect in a murder investigation? That'd be just too cool to keep under wraps. These are teenagers, remember. One of 'em would talk to a girl to impress her, and she'd get on the horn to her girlfriends, and so on. Believe me, we'd hear something, even if it was just a whisper."

Billboard had joined them from the kitchen, listening gravely as he wiped off his wet hands onto his apron. "It don't wash, if you ask me. Lookit, the kid's only been two places in his life, the old neighborhood and down south there in that little town near the abbey. If he ain't in either place, where the hell would he be?"

"There's that fantasy Joe told us about," Tomzak said. "How Sean and his buddy used to talk about driving out to California."

"Yeah, and that's what it sounds like to me, a fantasy. I mean, what'd he do, boost a car? C'mon, man. You know Sean. You see that kid takin' off on his own like that? He was too much a homeboy for that."

Greene said, "Murder's put the wanderlust into more than one kid."

Billboard pointed a finger at him. "That's the difference between you and me, man. You got the kid convicted on a murder rap already and I know he didn't do it. Sean Carpenter ain't no killer. So if you two are wrong about that, it stands to reason you're wrong about Sean not hiding out up along Backus Avenue somewhere. Which is why I'm heading back up there again this afternoon to find him."

"You better be damn careful up there," Hafner said. "You might find something you weren't looking for, you go messing too much with the Back Boys."

Reuben Macky, hiding his conflicting emotions as only an ex-con can, said, "Don't worry about us, man. Worry about those gangbangers."

*          *          *

"They're apt to bust their parole restrictions wide

open if they go rampaging up Backus Avenue like a couple of Rambos."

"Hey, we warned 'em. They're big boys. And Macky's done his parole, remember? He can cover Ralston's bony ass, take some heat for him if it comes to that." Hafner guided the Ford sedan through the intersection of Monroe and Colfax in the suburb of Densmore. "Anyhow, busting a few Back Boy heads shouldn't be a parole violation, it should be grounds for a citation from the mayor. Now, if you don't mind, could we get back to the case we're getting paid to investigate?"

"Hey, fine by me. We'd be there by now if you'd push this bucket a little. You'd think you were driving that RV of yours, the way you're dawdling along."

"Yeah, yeah." Hafner did not want to go there. Only that morning he and Marie had had yet another argument about his desire to buy a new and better camper. Forty-eight grand, plus a few bucks for extras and taxes; when she heard the price for the Coachman he had his eye on, she about hit the ceiling. "What about the kids' college funds? What about a pool for the backyard? What about that trip to Europe we've talked about for nearly twenty years?" On and on; she had a million reasons why a hard-working man shouldn't enjoy the fruits of his labor pursuing a personal passion.

But he was ready for her this time.

"The college funds are doing just fine, thanks to automatic monthly withdrawals from my paycheck *and*, if it's not enought to send two kids to Harvard, so be it. Face it, the Hafner offspring aren't exactly Ivy League material; they'll do just fine attending the state university system.

"The backyard pool, if you wanna talk about a waste of money, is the biggest waste of all, given that we've got only three good months when the temperatures get up into the eighties. And you know *damn well*, Marie, that you won't go near a pool if it's any cooler than that. Besides which, all the best campgrounds have big Olympic-size pools with triple diving boards and slides and everything. Now, if this global warming thing turns out to be true, maybe I'll reconsider."

And Europe, that was the easy one. "If you'll notice," he told her, "*you're* the one's been talking about a trip to Europe for the last however-many years, not me. Drafty castles and dingy old churches might be your idea of a good time, but if we put it to a family vote, both the kids would agree with me that they'd have more fun driving down to Orlando and staying at a deluxe RV campground near Disney World."

At which point, she had crossed her arms over those ample breasts of hers, set her jaw, narrowed her eyes at him, and said, "Do you have any idea how many vacations we can spend in deluxe *hotel* rooms, eating out at good restaurants instead of *me* having to slave over a twenty-inch range, with forty-eight thousand dollars? *Plus* the interest on the loan, which probably adds, what, another twenty or thirty thousand to the cost overall?"

"She's forgetting about the trade-in value of our Mallard," Hafner muttered. "The dealer offered me fifteen grand on that, so the loan's only thirty-three grand. And the Coachman comes with a microwave oven—"

"Hey!" Greene lightly swatted his arm. "What you mumbling about, partner?"

"Huh?" Hafner gripped the steering wheel at ten-and-two like a novice and sat up straighter. "Nothing. Just—daydreaming."

"Yeah, right. Too much partying at that wedding reception last night if you ask me." Greene got the needle out. "A man your age, you need all the rest you can get."

"It was a twenty-fifth anniversary party for my cousin and his wife. And nobody asked you."

"True."

They rode down Colfax in an easy silence for a few minutes, Hafner spotting the turnoff onto the Muncys' street a nanosecond before Greene raised his arm to point it out. The house on Waverly Terrace looked about as it had the day before. It was a rambling Cape Cod with gray shingles and a dark, steeply pitched roof with three dormers, an attached two-car garage, and a small but immaculately landscaped yard. The only difference was the blue Volvo sedan that sat somewhat akilter in the driveway; that hadn't been there on their last visit. Nor had the Metro Police cruiser that was parked at the curb.

The call had been routed to them while they were having coffee at The Hard Time Cafe. A patrolman in a cruiser, assigned to do a pass-by on the house each hour, had noted the appearance of the Volvo some twenty-five minutes ago. The car was registered to their missing murder suspect, Mrs. Susan Muncy. The detectives ordered the patrolman to keep an eye on the house, stop her if she tried to leave, but otherwise sit tight until they could make it out there themselves.

Hafner pulled in right behind the Volvo, blocking it, and Greene hopped out just before the Ford came to a dead stop. He walked out to the sidewalk to meet with the patrolman, who had gotten out of his car and was standing there with his hands resting on his crowded equipment belt.

"Any activity?" Greene asked him.

"Nothing I could make out, Sarge."

"Okay. Hang loose and keep an eye peeled in case she tries to sneak out a side exit."

He rejoined Hafner for a moment at the foot of the

front stoop, then circled around to the back of the house. Hafner waited for a twenty count, then went to the door. He stood sideways next to the jamb and rang the bell, his other hand inside his coat, resting on the nine millimeter he wore on his hip. It's not that he expected anything hinky to happen, but you never knew.

When there was no response to his second long ring of the bell, he called out her name—"Mrs. Muncy?"—and identified himself. Then he tried the doorknob.

Unlocked.

A deep breath. Then, "This is a police officer, Mrs. Muncy. I'm here to speak with you about your husband's death. I'm coming in now, ma'am."

Another deep breath, a push of the door, and he went in low, crouching beside the first object he came to—a grandfather clock in the foyer—giving his eyes a moment to adjust. He saw her almost immediately, down the hallway, through an arched doorway into the kitchen. She was sitting there at the kitchen table, in profile, still as a photograph.

He came slowly down the corridor, repeating his name and why he was there, glancing around for unexpected hazards: a guard dog, a lover with a gun. Nothing leaped out at him from the edges, and the woman at the table didn't move but enough to breathe. There was a purse on the table and a water glass, empty, in front of her. She was dressed in an expensive business suit, blue linen, heavily creased, and her short auburn hair looked matted in back.

"Mrs. Susan Muncy?"

He was beside her now. Outside, through French doors to the patio, was Greene. She looked up at Hafner, her brown eyes dull.

"I shot my husband," she said, her voice a croak. "Did you know? I killed Alan."

# CHAPTER
# 14

Billboard and Reuben Macky descended from the number ten bus onto the sidewalk at the corner of Backus Avenue and Arbutus Street. Both men wore the denims and thick-soled black shoes that made up part of the uniform worn by the staff of The Hard Time Cafe. Both had changed, however, from the telltale blue cotton work shirts with the names stenciled over the breast pocket. Billboard had on a black Harley-Davidson T-shirt under a lightweight windbreaker; Macky wore a yellow short-sleeved pullover that displayed his bulging biceps.

He looked around and said, "You ready, man?"

Billboard reflexively patted the compact lump in the pocket of the windbreaker. "Ready to rock and roll."

"Then let's go scare us up some Backus Avenue Boys."

\* \* \*

Back at the cafe, Chet Tomzak was hunched over the cashier's counter in front, the telephone handset pressed to his ear. "They left maybe half an hour ago," he said. "Right after the lunch crowd petered out. Not that it was much of a crowd. Slow day today, Father. I guess folks are out of town on vacations and such—"

"Yes, I imagine they are." Father Joe didn't mean to cut him off, but he had no patience for shop talk that day. "I appreciate their efforts. I only hope they don't get themselves into trouble. Dealing with Marco and his gang can be a tough assignment."

"Well, they're a couple of tough guys."

"Frankly, that's what worries me, that they'll do something wild—"

"I think Billboard has a plan, if that's any consolation. I saw him huddling with Sister Matty before he took off with Reuben."

"Well, that's somewhat reassuring. If they come up with anything at all on Sean, have them call me down here. You have the number?"

"Yes, Father, we have the number." Tomzak could hear the strain in the priest's voice. He wondered if he should even tell him about that morning's visit from the sergeants, then decided to tell him anyway. "Hafner and Greene were in for coffee. They did a little poking around up on Backus themselves and, uh, frankly, they don't think Sean's hiding out up there."

Father Joe sighed. "I've been beginning to have my own doubts." For a moment, the line went silent. Then, "Anyway, Chet, I really called to talk to you. I need some information about computers, specifically the setup they have down here at the abbey."

"Well, I'll help if I can, but I'm no expert." Joe and the others merely thought he was, because he knew his way around the computers at the rectory, in particular the

one in Father Joe's office. It was used to keep track of the
cafe's budget and inventory as well as the overall budget
for the various programs and operational expenses of
Corpus Christi. Tomzak had worked with similar
software programs as the manager of a tavern in his
previous life, prior to serving a prison term for vehicular
homicide. That and his advanced hunt-and-peck
keyboarding talents had gotten him assigned as the
church's resident computer specialist.

"What I need to know, Chet, is this: if a program or a
file is erased from the computer's memory, is there any
way to get it back again? Or at least to see if it was even
there in the first place?"

"Um, yeah, there are ways of doing that, sure. See,
when you delete a file from the computer's hard drive,
it doesn't literally mean the information is gone. Not in
most cases, anyway. All you've done is told the operating
system that it doesn't have to keep track of that file
anymore, so the space it takes up can be reused if
needed. Overwritten, it's called."

Father Joe was beginning to perk up. "So if something
was there, it's still there? Somewhere?"

Tomzak chuckled. "Well, yeah. It should be. Unless—"

A groan came down the phone line. "Unless what?"

"Unless the hard drive is near capacity, in which case
the system will literally erase deleted files to make room
for new files. In that case, I think you're out of luck."

"All right, well, assuming the hard drive isn't near
capacity," Father Joe said, "could you search it for recently
deleted files? I mean, if you drove down here and—"

"Whoa. You're asking the wrong guy. I don't know that
much about it, except in theory. I'd have to go over to
the computer store and talk to somebody knowledgeable,

see if they have an app I could use—"

"An app?"

"An application. A utility-type program I could use to run a search on the hard drive." Tomzak exhaled. "Look, what you really need isn't me, Father, it's the guy I'd be talking to at the computer store. A hacker who knows this stuff inside and out. Preferably a seventeen-year-old nerd who—hey! Like that kid you told us about last night, that friend of Sean's."

"Mike Keller," Father Joe said, shaking his head at his own stupidity. "Of course."

\*   \*   \*

It took less time to make contact the second time around, thanks to a tip inadvertently dropped by Sergeants Hafner and Greene that morning. They now knew about the abandoned house on Wakeland, a former crack house that served as the informal headquarters of the Backus Avenue Boys. Twenty minutes after arriving at the sagging stoop of the house, smoking a couple of Kools each while they loitered in plain sight, Macky and Billboard were rewarded with a visit by half a dozen red-jacketed Back Boys. They seemed to materialize like ghosts, slipping out from around the corners of the boarded-up house and forming a half-circle around the two ex-cons.

"What the fuck you guys think you're doin'?"

The spokesman was the same tall, red-haired, pasty-faced punk who'd done the talking in the alley the previous day. Right next to him was the same short, broad black kid with the stone face and the vacant eyes, the one who liked to strop the blade of his flick-knife on the sleeve of his jacket. Only there were no knives showing today, this close to home. Instead, each of the six had a hand in the pocket of his jacket, sending the message without actually flashing the steel.

"We need to talk to Marco," Billboard said. "We found out some stuff he'd wanna know, see, and I figure he might like to work a swap, like."

"Marco don't want you hangin' out front here. We been gettin' enough heat, all the fuckin' cops been comin' around, but you guys ain't cops. You two assholes we don't have to put up with."

Macky bristled at the insult but kept his anger in check. "So take us to see Marco," he said with a shrug. "We have a little chat, see if we can do each other some good. Then me and my bud here go back where we came from. Problem solved."

"Yeah," Billboard said. "Save an ugly scene right out here on the sidewalk. All that's bound to get you is more cops."

They watched as the redhead thought about it. It wasn't his strong suit, thinking, which is what they'd been counting on. When the brain started cramping up on the little creep, he'd look to bump the problem along to a higher authority. And that's what he did.

"C'mon, then," he said finally. "We'll let Marco straighten out you two assholes."

\*    \*    \*

Marco Pilato sat on a fat upholstered chair raised up on a packing crate, like some middle-eastern potentate holding court. Except that the gold brocade of the chair was worn and patched in spots and it looked like it had been picked up off the curb on trash day. And the surroundings weren't any better.

They were gathered in what once would've been the living room of the house, back in the days when Wakeland Street was still a decent residential street of modest houses and blue-collar workers. But that was decades ago now, before the clothing factories had shut down and moved overseas and the small tool-and-die shops had fled to suburban industrial parks. Before the flowery paper on the living room walls had yellowed and faded and peeled, before the graffiti and the random fist-sized holes in the plaster had been added.

It was a small room to begin with. Billboard's and particularly Macky's bulk seemed to shrink it down to the size of a walk-in closet. Marco Pilato stared in silence at the two men while the punk with the red hair whispered in his ear. Then, in a sullen, hoarse voice, he dismissed most of the troops that had crowded in around them. Only the redhead and his sidekick, the dead-eyed black kid, stayed.

"We be right outside, you need us," said one of the departing gangbangers, a skinny Latino no more than fourteen years old.

"It's cool, man," Marco said. "These old guys ain't lookin' for trouble. Are you?"

"Nope," Billboard said, smiling. "Only for a few answers."

Marco Pilato was maybe nineteen, a lean six-footer with short, wavy dark hair, an olive complexion, and narrow eyes. His face might've been considered handsome if not for the acne scars that pitted his cheeks and the perpetual sneer.

He leaned forward, resting an elbow on each knee of his baggy jeans. "My boy says you got some information to trade. Start talkin'. I like what I hear, maybe we won't have to slice up your bad asses."

On cue, the redhead and his stocky associate pulled knives from the back pockets of their jeans and flicked them open. Big Red's face remained impassive but the black kid couldn't conceal his glee. *Just like the last time,* Macky thought. *He wants to cut somebody.*

Billboard held up his palms and said soothingly, "Now, now."

Macky looked over at him. "Now?"

"Yeah. Now."

Macky spun on his left heel and dropped the stocky gangbanger with a crunching right to the mouth, then pivoted the rest of the way around, completing the circle by planting his left elbow on the side of Big Red's face. The black kid went down hard and stayed down, but the redhead still had some juice left. He got his balance and swung the knife in an arc, hoping to gut Macky, but Macky jumped back. As the kid's arm swung past, Macky stepped in and sent a straight right hand to Big Red's jaw. That time he went down for good.

In the three seconds it took Macky to disable the two gangbangers, Billboard corraled Marco Pilato with a headlock and dragged him down off his throne. He half dragged, half kicked him over to the wall and proceeded to use his face to sand off some of the loose wallpaper.

"Whose ass you gonna slice now, you little pisspot? Huh? I oughta shove that blade down your throat, boy. Sideways. Little punk bastard."

"Ask your questions, hillbilly," Macky said, picking up the knives from the floor. "I'll take the door, but make it quick, man. We ain't got all day."

"You damn right you don't!" Pilato grunted, struggling uselessly against Billboard's hold. "My boys gonna storm back in here and carve you up—"

"Yeah, and find their fearless leader gettin' an ass whippin' from an 'old man.' You want 'em to see how easy you are, Marco, whinin' like some butt boy? Or you wanna tell me what I wanna know?"

"Fuck you, man!" He tried to yell out, but Billboard

banged his face back into the plaster, splitting his lip open in the process. "Ow! Jesus Christ—"

"Now, now, no takin' the Lord's name in vain," Billboard said, tightening his choke hold. "Sister Matty wouldn't approve. Now, are you about ready to answer some questions, butt boy?"

Pilato grunted a string of nonsense, earning him another painful encounter with the wall.

"All I wanna hear from you, son, is nice, short answers. Yes sir, no sir. Like that." Billboard swiftly swung the kid around and put him back-first against the wall, at the same time shoving his forearm up under his chin. "Now, do you have Sean Carpenter?"

"Nnnn-no!" Marco's eyes were swimming in their sockets.

"I think you're lying, son," Billboard said, leaning harder against the kid's windpipe.

"Nnnn-no! Uh-uhh, pleej."

The ex-con, ex-biker enforcer eased off a tad, allowing the kid to swallow a little air. Macky was in the foyer, sneaking peeks out at the street through a crack in the door. Marco's two lieutenants were moaning, starting to stir ever so slightly.

Marco gulped a couple of times. "I got no idea what's up with Carp, man. I'm tellin' it straight. Yeah, I tried to get him back with the Boys, but he had his own thing goin' and that's cool."

"Yeah, I'm sure. You just decided to forget about gettin' him back up here to run some computer scam for you." Billboard gave him a taste of the forearm again.

"No, man! Listen, okay? I wanted Carp back, yeah, but I figured I'd get to him later, in the fall, man, when he comes up here to start school at Riverton Tech. I wasn't gonna kidnap him from no bunch a monks."

Billboard was six inches away, staring into Pilato's eyes. He saw fear there, but did he see truth? He was still trying to make up his mind when the leader of the Backus Avenue Boys decided it for him.

"Look, man, on my grandmother's grave, we ain't seen Carp since me and Blood drove down there to Garfield last week to try and talk some trash with the dude. He turned us down flat, man. Said he had his own thing happenin', was gonna blow the whistle on somebody was runnin' some kinda computer scam a their own down there at that monastery. Carp, he figured he might get a reward or somethin'. I tried tellin' him that'd be like chump change, man, but—"

"Who was it? You mean the monk he was working for, Brother John?"

"I dunno, man, I guess so. Somethin' about that bread operation they got down there, is all I know."

Macky whistled softly from the foyer. "The natives are getting restless." The two on the floor were coming around now, working their way up to hands and knees, heads still hung low and groggy. "I think it's time to execute part B of the plan, man."

"Yeah." Billboard stared into Marco Pilato's eyes again, knowing he'd heard the truth this time. He pushed him away.

Marco stumbled, then righted himself. "Now what, asshole?" he rasped, fingers kneading his raw throat. "Think you two are just gonna walk outa here—?"

"Something like that." Billboard reached into the pocket of his windbreaker and brought out the compact cell phone he'd borrowed from Sister Matty. He flipped it open and punched in three numbers: 911.

# CHAPTER
## 15

Father Joe Costello guided his Honda Civic along Garfield's Main Street, craning his neck to look up at the signs on the old-fashioned buildings. Mrs. Keller had described the computer shop as a back-alley hole-in-the-wall between the drugstore and Brown's Hardware. He spotted the hardware store first, thanks to a collection of wheelbarrows and lawn mowers that were lined up on the sidewalk in front. Next came Rexall Drugs. The two buildings were separated by a service alley.

He angled the car into the first available space he came to, a block down from the drugstore, and backtracked. The alley was narrower than he'd first estimated, obviously just a pedestrian shortcut to the real service alley running behind the buildings. But he could see a couple of doors down there, one of which had a sign jutting out above it that read ARV Electronics.

A bell jangled when he entered, bringing a young man

of about thirty out from the backroom. He was tall and
heavy through the middle, with long brown hair that
hung limp over his forehead and was pinned behind his
ears with the aid of his thick glasses. He wore baggy jeans
and an oversized T-shirt adorned with a decal of a shirt
and tie. Casual was the watchword for the shop too.
Everywhere Father Joe looked in the cramped space,
including atop the counter that separated customer from
shopkeeper, he saw stacks of electronic gear, old and new.

"Uh, help you with something, Father?"

"You must be Andy Vandy."

"Guilty. Andy Vandemere, actually, but the kids all call
me Andy Vandy."

Father Joe nodded. "It's one of the local kids who
brings me by. Mike Keller. His mother thought he might
be here—"

"Oh, sure, he's in back doing some installation work
for me. C'mon."

Father Joe followed the man's lead through the bead
curtain and into a workshop that was at least three times
the size of the front room. High workbenches built
crudely of two-by-fours and plywood rimmed three
walls. Shelving underneath the benches was crowded
with monitors and CPUs and peripherals, but the
benchtop itself was relatively uncluttered.

Mike Keller was seated on a high stool, his slight frame
bent over an open computer case. A gooseneck lamp
with a round fluorescent lightbulb glowed next to his left
shoulder. He didn't look up from his work.

"Hey, Mikey. You got a visitor," Andy Vandy said.

"Yeah?" Still, he remained hunched over the computer
case, intent on what he was doing. Father Joe took his
cue from Andy and waited silently. After another ten

seconds, the teenager said, "Ahh, got the bastard pinned," and looked up. The smile of triumph on his face immediately melted away at the sight of the priest.

"Oh, Father, hi. I was, like, having a bear of a time getting a new video card to slot into this baby."

"But you finally got the bastard pinned, huh?" Father Joe said with a small grin.

"Yeah." Mike laughed. He spun around on the stool and propped his sneakers on the supports. "You're looking for me, huh? Something about Sean?"

"Yes. I'm sorry to disturb you, but I have some questions about Sean's work at the abbey, the computer programming he'd been doing, and I thought you might be able to help me out."

The boy's eyes grew wide at the mention of computers. "Yeah, sure, Father, if I can. What d'ya need to know?"

Father Joe pulled out one of the other stools and sat down across from Mike. Andy Vandy found a clear section of workbench and leaned against it, arms crossed over his chest.

"Well, the last time we talked," Father Joe said, "you mentioned that Sean might've had something on Brother John. Something that he could use to 'take him down a peg.' You remember?"

"Sure, only Sean never told me what it was."

"But did he tell you whether it was something he'd learned while programming the abbey's new business software? Something in one of the files he'd been working with?"

The boy thought about it for a moment. "No, he didn't come out and say it was anything he'd gotten from the machine—but that's what I assumed he meant. I mean, that's what Sean did, right? He was a computer geek, like me and Andy." This was said with pride and a touch of arrogance; geekdom, apparently, was a desired status in some circles.

Father Joe was ready to accept Mike Keller's intuition about Sean because it matched his own. Not that such assumptions would impress the Lorret County Sheriff's Department or its lead investigator, Sergeant Podesta. Naturally, to get the sergeant to pay attention, he'd need something tangible. Some solid evidence that Sean Carpenter had found some bit of information stored away in the abbey's computer system that had somehow created a crisis situation—a situation that had ended in murder.

"That's just what I need, Mike," he said. "A first-rate computer geek to come over to the abbey and run a thorough search of their PC's hard drive. You think you can help me out?"

"Yeah, probably. I mean, I'd love to give it a try, Father," the boy said. "What're we looking for anyway?"

"I don't really know," Father Joe admitted. "I'm hoping one of us will recognize it—whatever *it* is—when we see it."

*       *       *

While Father Costello was down in Garfield rounding up Mike Keller, Sergeant Podesta was working the car radio from the abbey grounds. Standing beside the unmarked county car was Father Mazewski, looking commanding and stern in his flowing habit. And more than a little agitated, as well.

"Sergeant, are you absolutely certain this is necessary?"

Podesta leaned and swung his head outside the open car door—"Absolutely."—and then leaned back in and barked more orders into the radio's handmike.

But the abbot, a former attorney, wasn't the sort to

surrender to a policeman's agenda quite that easily. "But scuba divers and boats with drag lines—have you any idea how disruptive this investigation of yours is becoming?"

Podesta looked up at him but continued talking on the radio. When he finished, he signed off, then pushed himself up out of the car and casually rested his arms along the top of the car door.

"Define *disruptive* for me, Father," he said, the levelness of his tone masking the anger he felt welling up inside. "I mean, on a scale of ten, where would you rank the aggravation factor of my investigation? For example, is it slightly above or slightly below the disruption Brother John caused by turning up murdered on your garden path?"

For the briefest moment, Podesta saw past the abbot's steel-framed glasses into the depths of his steely gray eyes. What he saw there was anger, directed straight at him, and Podesta felt seared by it as only a public servant can. But, like a lightning strike, the abbot's anger quickly dissipated, leaving behind a vapor of irritation.

"That's not fair, Sergeant. I've tried to help you do your job however I could—no one is more interested in finding the answers to this tragedy than I. But unlike you, I can't put all my focus on a murder investigation. I owe something to the other thirty-five men who live at this abbey. I have to be concerned with our mission here, and frankly, having more and more police and emergency vehicles showing up here is *extremely* disruptive. In addition to the state of mind of the brothers, there's this evening's memorial to Brother John to consider. Many people from outside the abbey will be attending, and I don't know where they're going to park—"

"Park?" This was about parking? Podesta shook his head. He didn't get these people and he never would. Still, the sheriff wouldn't like getting an unhappy phone call from a prominent citizen of Lorret County, particularly not on a weekend.

The sergeant took a deep breath and exhaled slowly. "Look, Father, with any luck I'll have the divers and the drag boat in and outa here in two hours. The pond isn't that big."

"But are you sure it's necessary—?"

"I'm not sure of anything, Father Mazewski, except that, when in doubt, I'm usually better off following my instincts. My instincts tell me that, bad eyes or not, Brother Jerome saw someone messing around down in those woods and around that pond two nights ago and it wasn't Smokey the Bear."

Even an old prosecutor knew badgering a witness would take you only so far. The abbot conceded with a slump of the shoulders, adding, "But you'll be done by four or so, is that right?"

Podesta laughed, because it was his best alternative. "If you don't mind my asking, Father, how'd you get this job anyway? I mean, does the Pope or something appoint you—?"

"No, no. Although, I *am* elected, just like His Holy Father. Only, whereas His Holiness is elected by the College of Cardinals, an abbot is chosen by a vote of the permanent monks, those who've taken their perpetual vows."

"You mean you have to run for office, just like a congressman or something?"

"It's not so much that you run for the office, more like the office chooses you. And a better analogy would be the Senate, since we at the Abbey of the Ganannoqua serve six-year terms."

Podesta shook his head. He should've known. Everywhere you look, it's nothing but politics.

# CHAPTER 16

The machine was an IBM with a 233-Pentium processor, a 2.5 gigabyte hard drive, and a seventeen-inch Sony monitor. There were a few peripherals too, in addition to the ink jet printer, but Mike hadn't bothered to describe any of those, so Father Joe was largely in the dark as to their functions. Watching the sixteen-year-old self-titled nerd work the keyboard like Glenn Gould merely reinforced the priest's feelings of uselessness in all things digital.

On the other hand, he consoled himself, Mike Keller probably didn't know the first thing about the Holy Scriptures and the liturgy.

"Well, Father, there's still plenty of space left on the drive."

"That's good, right?"

"Right. Means it hasn't had to overwrite deleted files."

"Oh." Father Joe blinked. More gobbledygook came up on the screen. "Okay."

Suddenly the young computer whiz sat back in the chair, still keeping his eyes trained on the monitor. "Whoa!"

"Whoa?

"You like to fish, Father?"

"I've been known to wet a line when I can find the time."

"Well, I just got a nibble, okay? It didn't take my bobber all the way under, but it was a pretty solid hit. I'd say we got a lunker or two swimming just below the surface."

While Father Joe's brain was downloading and analyzing the metaphor, Mike slipped a disk from the external drive he'd hooked up to the PC. He tossed that disk aside and took another from the bundle in his nylon pack and inserted that into the "x-drive," as he called it.

"Need something a little bigger to crunch this baby." He glanced up at the priest. "Changing bait."

"Right."

Father Joe straightened and flexed at the hips, trying to work out the stiffness that had crept into his backbone. He'd been hunched over Mike's shoulder for twenty minutes, hardly breathing as he watched his wizard fingers fly. Strings of nonsense words and numerals rolled across the monitor in seemingly endless waves, the boy grunting at each new surge. It might just as well have been Chinese ideograms for all Father Joe could make of it.

"See, what we have here," Mike said, as if reading Father Joe's thoughts, "is basically an S&R program on the floppy—"

"S&R?"

"Search and rescue. It's doing a segment search of the

hard drive, looking for submerged files. Files that are still in there but no longer recognized with file names."

"Sort of like the subconscious mind," the priest said. "Information the brain has suppressed, pushed off into a corner somewhere."

"Right. Something like that." Mike made a few more rapid keystrokes. "Only this stuff isn't really hidden in a corner; it's right where it's always been, just unlabeled. That's where the rescue part comes in. With any luck—there!"

A blue box appeared on the screen, with a message centered in it. The message said: 79 DELETED FILES FOUND.

"Seventy-nine!" Father Joe gasped. "Somebody's erased, or attempted to erase, seventy-nine files?"

"That's not unusual, Father. I mean, I open files all the time and later delete them. Everybody does. Letters you don't need to save, a temporary back-up file, or a batch file. Seventy-nine is no big deal."

Father Joe suppressed a groan. "It is when you're looking for a needle in a haystack, and you don't even know what the needle looks like. If they're unlabeled, doesn't that mean you'll have to try and recall all seventy-nine files, so we can read through them—?"

"Not necessarily. Not if we can narrow down our search some."

"And how would we do that?"

The boy shrugged his bony shoulders. "Use search criteria like dates. Only access files that were opened or deleted within the past two weeks, say. Or we could search only for data files, as opposed to document files. Or vice versa—"

Father Joe clapped him on the back. "Mike, you're

a gift from heaven."

"Ah, jeez," he said, turning crimson. But his fingers kept moving across the keyboard.

A minute later, Brother Malthius came in. "I'm sorry to interrupt, Father, but a phone call came in for you up at the abbot's office. You can take it down here if you like. It's, uh, someone named—Billboard? Does that sound right?"

\*     \*     \*

It was a hot day, the bugs were out, and the pond had a stagnant, gassy smell about it. Stirring it up with all this activity wasn't helping matters. Already the two divers had reported that trying to see anything down there was like staring through pea soup. Sergeant Podesta didn't want to hear about it.

"Feel around. Use your flashlights. You're getting paid to do a job, aren't you? So go do it."

But after the first twenty minutes, they hadn't found a thing in Mary's Pond, not even the usual assortment of empty cans and bottles. This was a monastery, after all, not some county park hangout for teenagers and picnicking families.

Podesta didn't mind. If he had to guess, based on what he'd learned from the latest updates from the M.E., he'd bet the murder weapon probably never made it down to the grotto, let alone got thrown into the pond. It was definitely a bread knife, most likely taken from the bakery. If the killer had any brains at all, he'd probably slipped the bloody knife into the big industrial dishwasher they used over there, along with all the other dirty knives, and that was that.

So the scuba team was mostly a procedure thing— something for Podesta to do so that later no one could say he *didn't* do it. A CYA move—cover your ass.

The more interesting prospect, Podesta believed, lay with the drag boat. It was a fourteen-foot aluminum skiff powered by a seven-horsepower trolling motor that would push it along at a top speed of about five knots. No good for towing skiers along a white-capped lake, but perfect for towing the dragnet methodically across a meadow pond. Two of the deputies had driven it down to the site along a tractor lane, backing the boat trailer as close to the edge of the pond as was safe. Despite the deputies' assurances that they could handle the launch themselves, Podesta had donned a pair of yellow waders and had carefully waded out into the sloping muck to help them guide the skiff into the murky water.

He was still standing there, five feet off-shore and knee-deep in muck, when Brother Chan arrived.

"Sergeant?" Chan called from the path. "I understand you wanted to see me?"

Podesta kept his eyes trained on the drag boat for another thirty seconds, watching as it moved methodically left to right—west to east—across the far shore of Mary's Pond. Then he turned halfway, sloshing water over his boot tops and almost losing his balance.

"Yeah, uh, Brother. I have a question or two I thought you might be able to help me with. But first—" A sheepish grin split the investigator's face. "—you think you might be able to give me a hand up outa here? I seem to be stuck in the mud."

"Certainly," Chan said, sounding anything but certain. He walked down the grassy slope between the path and the pond, carefully picking his steps at the water's edge. With his right foot planted gingerly but firmly on a half-submerged rock, he reached for and grasped Podesta's outstretched hand. "Careful now, don't pull too har—ahh!"

"Sorry." Podesta's initial grab had almost pulled the

slim monk into the water. "Take another grip and pull back slowly."

Brother Chan's right hand wrapped itself in Podesta's right hand. This time Podesta let the monk do all the pulling, but it was no go. Brother Chan wasn't strong enough to budge the stocky policeman from the muddy water.

"Well—push off a bit with your legs, Sergeant," Chan groaned through clenched teeth. "I can't do it alone."

"Oh. Good idea. What was I thinking?" Podesta curled up his toes inside his left boot and pulled it up out of the muck with a great sucking sound. Once it was planted on a submerged rock, he was able to do the same with the other foot. "For a second there, I thought I was going to lose the county a good pair of boots," he said, tramping up onto solid ground.

Brother Chan, breathing hard, rested his hands on the knees of his smock. Between breaths he said, "You'd think all the labor we do in the fields would make a man fit for anything, wouldn't you? I must be getting old."

"Nah, I'm just too fat, is all."

Podesta moved over to the boat trailer and pulled off the muddy waders. Brother Chan waited until he was through and had returned the boots to the back of the county four-by-four the trailer was hitched to.

"You had more questions, Sergeant?"

"Right. I hope I didn't take you away from anything too important."

"Important, but not pressing. I was reviewing a reading assignment with a couple of our novitiates up in the library."

"Ah, that's right. You're the abbey's—what is it?"

"Novice master. Among other duties."

"Right. Well, I won't keep you long." Podesta hesitated. "These novitiates of yours, they're young men mostly? Some boys, even, around Sean Carpenter's age?"

"At the present time, they range in age from nineteen to fifty. We have only three novices under twenty-five, with the majority in their thirties or older. It's often the case that our novices come here later in life, after having worked in some career in the secular world."

"Uh-huh." Podesta searched his brain for another question. "Um, were any of the novices particularly close to Sean? I mean, did he hang out with any of them at all? Share an interest, like in cars or computers or girls? Well, not girls, I guess, but—"

Chan frowned. "The answer is no, Sergeant. First, our novitiates have precious little time to 'hang out.' And if they did, I doubt it would be with Sean. Sean, as I've explained to you, is an agnostic. The men who come here to join us in the Trappist life are committed to their faith. There's not much common ground, even in instances where the ages are similar."

"Okay." Podesta shrugged. "So what you're saying is I'd probably be wasting my time if I talked to any of the young novices, looking for something on the Carpenter kid."

"It's my understanding that you or one of your men has already spoken with each of them, Sergeant. Along with everyone else in this monastery."

"That's true, but we always do follow-ups. Anyway, I guess that's all, Brother. Thanks for your time."

Chan stared at him a moment. "That's all?"

"That's all. Thanks."

The sergeant watched the perplexed monk walk back up the grotto path toward the woods and the abbey complex beyond. Then he turned his attention back to the drag boat. They were in the middle of the pond now, put-putting towards his end, one of the deputies working the stick while the other kept the dragnet fed out straight.

Podesta wiped his brow and reached for his shirt pocket, remembering at the last moment that he couldn't smoke on abbey grounds. *Damn it.* He hated that about himself, that he had a habit with that kind of hold on him. Powerful enough to push him outdoors into an alley in the dead of winter or keep him from going to see overly long movies.

"Stinkin' goddamn cancer sticks," he muttered. He reached into his pants pocket and took out a stick of gum, stripped it, folded it into his mouth, and chewed furiously.

It didn't help. God, he needed a cigarette. Well, look for a silver lining. It was hotter than hell out, and the meadow was covered with dry grass. Maybe it would spontaneously combust into a grass fire, and he'd be able to stand there and breathe in some of the secondhand smoke.

Jesus, he was pathetic.

He was thinking of adding a second piece of spearmint to the one in his mouth when one of the deputies on the boat, Streb, shouted.

"What? You got something?" Podesta duckwalked down the slope to the pond's edge. The skiff was only about twenty feet off-shore now. Streb was standing up, his legs straddling the center thwart, pulling in the line on the dragnet.

"Yeah, Sarge, shit, and it's solid too. Take us in to shore, Jake."

While Streb kept slowly reeling in the net, straining until the veins of his neck were ready to pop, the other deputy steered to the bank. With Podesta's help he beached the skiff's bow. Then all three men took lines and, hand over hand, brought in the net. As their catch came up into shallower water, it bounced on the submerged rocks and rolled over. Suddenly, breaking the surface of the green murk was a face.

"Oh, Jesus Christ, Sarge! Yech!"

It wasn't much of a face anymore. In only two days, the snapping turtles and the crayfish and the other scavengers of the pond had found it easy pickings. But still, there was enough left for Podesta to whisper, "I think we've found our missing boy."

# CHAPTER 17

While his counterpart with
the Lorret County Sheriff's Department was dragging
Mary's Pond for answers to the Brother John murder,
Sergeant Hafner of the Riverton Metro Police was about
to close what he'd come to think of as the blue camper
case. For that reason alone, he should've been feeling
upbeat, but he wasn't. Somewhere in the back of his
mind, he suspected the case was ready to turn and bite
him like a rabid dog on a long leash.

He was standing just outside the interview room,
looking through the one-way glass at the woman seated
at the table, Mrs. Alan Muncy. Susan. Sitting stiffly at the
trestle table, the fingers of her right hand absently
twisting the wedding band on her left ring finger. She
wasn't much older than Hafner's wife; late forties, stylish
without being faddish, still a few years and a couple of
dress sizes short of matronly. Nervous, yes, but not overly.
Staring myopically at the mirrored wall when she wasn't

exchanging banalities with the female officer assigned to sit in there with her.

Sergeant Greene came down the corridor whistling something Top Forty and tuneless. A redundancy, Hafner decided. "What's the ADA got to say?"

Greene shrugged. The assistant district attorney, as usual, had sat firmly on the fence. "He says it's up to us. The woman waived her right to an attorney, so we can go ahead and question her even if it is a capital offense. But he also thinks it'd be better if we waited for him *and* Mrs. Muncy's lawyer to come down."

Hafner snorted. "Huh, what's that mean? Another hour or two before the ADA gets here? And who knows how long before this woman can get ahold of a lawyer herself? She's already copped. I say we formalize it now while she's still in a confessional mood. She gets used to the situation—who knows?"

Greene tended to agree with him. "But if she tips, wants a lawyer, we gotta shut down, Harold. The minute she asks."

Hafner glanced through the window again. "Let's just get this over with."

*       *       *

"Where'd you get the gun, Mrs. Muncy?"

The question was posed in an offhand manner, but it was the most important question of the day. Establish premeditation first and the rest is painting by numbers.

"From him. My husband. Alan."

Greene inched forward. "Your husband bought you the gun, ma'am? For protection, like that?"

She nodded. "I work late sometimes at the bank. It's in the suburbs, but still, there've been a few incidents in recent years. Muggings in the parking lot mostly."

"You were at work yesterday morning, Mrs. Muncy." Hafner, standing, slowly moved around to the opposite side of the table, between her and the mirrored wall. "But you drove into the city on your lunch hour. To talk to your husband, you said."

"Yes. I just needed to *talk*—"

"But you brought along the gun."

"What? Yes. I mean, I always have it, in my purse. It was Alan's idea—"

"There was trouble in the marriage, Mrs. Muncy? Things had come to a boil, is that it?"

"No. *No*—not like you mean."

"But *something* was bothering you," Hafner insisted. "I mean, enough so you'd drive all this way on your lunch hour to talk to Alan. And to take the gun along—"

"I told you, the gun was just there, in my purse. I didn't *take it*—"

"All right, ma'am." Greene again, softly. "You just relax, okay? And tell us what happened in your own words."

She was still glaring up at Hafner. Greene thought they had blown it; the woman would decide she wanted to wait for the lawyer after all and they'd be stuck in that stale little I-room until midnight, observing the legal niceties.

Wouldn't change much in the end, though. They already had her on tape, listening to Hafner repeat the Miranda, repeating again that she understood her rights. Saying it again, flat out, "I shot my husband. That's all."

But now she was balking, upset by his partner's lack of tact. Greene rebuked Hafner with a minute head shake, then prompted the woman again.

"In your own words, Susan. Take your time."

She pulled her gaze off Hafner, looked down at her

worrying fingers, then heaved a sigh that seemed to deflate the padded shoulders of her suit jacket.

Presently, she said, "Well, it was all because of that stupid camper—" Hafner suppressed a groan and an incipient case of deja vu. "—which *I* never wanted in the first place."

A midlife crisis, she called it. They'd been drifting for some time, she and Alan—getting along, but drifting apart somehow. For years their lives had centered around their daughter, Sonya, but she was away at college now—

"Oh, God, how can I explain this to her? I've been in a daze, driving around all night, and I never even thought what all this will do to Sonya."

"We'll deal with all that later, Susan," Greene told her, keeping it low-key. "Right now you have to help us understand what went down out there yesterday, okay? You said you and Alan were having problems . . ."

"Not problems, really. I mean, we weren't arguing— just the opposite. It was more like we'd run out of things to say to each other."

Alan seemed to sense it too, she said, because about a year ago, he suddenly got it into his head that they should become weekend campers. *Campers*—after twenty years of marriage and knowing how she feels about bugs and confined spaces. But he insisted it was just the ticket for their predictable, stressful lives—a couple of days a week relaxing among the quiet of tall trees and gurgling streams, et cetera. She'd learn to love it, he told her.

"The next thing I know," Mrs. Muncy continued, her green eyes still wide at the wonder of it, "he trades in the Taurus wagon for this great, lumbering Winnebago. The only way he could justify the expense, you see, is to have it double as his commuter car. For God's sake, it's twenty-two feet long, gets maybe eight miles to the gallon—well, you've seen it, sitting out there like Paul Bunyan's great blue ox. It's ridiculous, driving back and forth to work in that thing, paying double to park it—"

Hafner, who could contain himself no longer, blurted, "Maybe your husband figured the tax advantage offset all the bother." He reflexively rubbed at the grumbling in his stomach. "The IRS considers RV's like a second home—anything that has toilet facilities on board, in fact. So the interest on the payments is all deductible." The looks he was getting from both his partner and Mrs. Muncy convinced him to let the subject drop with a sheepish shrug.

"In any case, ma'am," Greene said, now glaring at Hafner himself, "your husband went out and bought this RV, spent a lot of money against your will—"

"I tried to make the best of it, I really did. Ask my friends, the people I work with down at the bank—"

They would certainly ask her friends and co-workers about a lot of things.

"—they'll tell you I tried. All through last summer and early fall, at least twice a month, we'd leave right after work on a Friday afternoon and drive up to Hamlin Beach State Park, or sometimes down to Stony Brook, and spend the whole weekend living out of that damned *camper*." Her lips twisted into a grimace, as if merely saying the word left a bitter aftertaste in her mouth. "Raining half the time, stuck inside a big tin can, eating out of little tin cans, even sleeping like a tin can, crammed into that overhead bunk hardly bigger than a pantry shelf. And worse, when the weather was good, what did we ever do but sit around in lawn chairs making small talk with people we didn't even know, enormous women in shower togs and one-size-fits-all caftans, men who never took off their baseball caps."

The tirade ended in a shudder.

Hafner, who was personally very fond of Hamlin Beach, managed to maintain his professionalism this time. "So it began eating away at you, is that right, ma'am? All those weekend trips—?"

She nodded vigorously. "But I put up with it." For the sake of the marriage, she said, she did her best to try and get into the spirit, all through that miserable, endless summer and fall; praying for winter to come so she wouldn't have to go anymore, and so that just maybe Alan would grow tired of piloting that barge back and forth to the city every day on slushy, snowbank-narrowed streets.

"I wanted it to be his idea, you see. A thousand times I thought about confronting him, giving him an ultimatum— but I couldn't do that to him. Anyway, I truly *believed* he'd gotten this RV business out of his system. I mean, all winter long he never once mentioned camping—not a word. But he didn't say anything about getting rid of the behemoth, either. So I finally did myself."

"You told your husband to sell the RV, Mrs. Muncy?"

"I *asked* him to *consider* selling it. With the money we'd save on the payments and operating costs, we could afford real vacations at a luxury resort someplace."

Hafner gnawed pensively at his lower lip; Greene picked up for him. "But Alan refused?"

She slowly rolled shut her eyes, then opened them and looked beseechingly at Greene. "I couldn't believe it. It was like all of a sudden he's the happy camper again. Telling me how much he was looking forward to another fun-filled summer in our little house on wheels." Her fingers raked the Formica tabletop before curling in on themselves.

"And this conversation occurred when, ma'am?"

"When? Oh, about a week ago."

Greene snuck a glance at his partner, both men thinking the same word: premeditation.

"Is that when you first decided to—take action?"

"I didn't decide anything at the time. I was too stunned, too depressed to even think." Then she caught the implication and sat up straight. "I already *told* you people, I didn't *plan* to shoot my husband—"

"Come on, lady." Hafner stepped up to the table and leaned over on his spread palms, angrier than he intended, his face a foot from hers. "You stewed over it for a week, getting madder and madder—"

"Yes, but—"

"—until today you finally worked up enough rage at the poor sap to drive all the way downtown on your lunch hour, *with* a .32 concealed in your purse—"

"I *always* carry the gun. I mean, I didn't even think about it. It was just there! I was angry, yes, and I was going to give Alan an ultimatum—me or his precious RV—but I never, ever thought about killing him."

"Oh, really? You show up mad as hell, packing a gun. You lure your husband out to the Winnebago—why didn't you meet in his office if all you had in mind was just to talk?"

"I didn't lure him anywhere! He was already there!" A sob caught in her throat, and then she swallowed and her voice leveled off to a precise, precarious calm. "I parked my car and was walking through the parking lot, intending to go up to Alan's office and invite him out for a surprise lunch—somewhere we could talk. I could see the RV up ahead of me, standing out like a beached whale. I was probably still about fifty feet away when the door swung open and *she* came sashaying out."

Hafner frowned and pulled back; Greene edged forward. "She, ma'am?"

"Polly." Susan Muncy spat out the name. "My husband's flashy little administrative assistant. The one he hired last year—just a few weeks before he was smitten with the camping bug." She looked up at Hafner and held him fast with the quiet fury in her eyes. "I watched her walk away, swinging her little size-six butt, back toward my husband's building. Then I marched up to the RV and threw open the door—and there was Alan, his shirttail still hanging out, folding the sleeping couch back into place. You mentioned rage, Sergeant? Yes. In that moment, the pain, the humiliation of it became rage. All those lost weekends in that stifling camper, pasting on a goddamn smiley face, being the good little wife—so that smug *bastard* could supply himself with a rolling motel room for his bimbo."

Exhausted, she added, "I don't even remember taking the gun out. It just happened. And that's the truth."

\*   \*   \*

Later, at the water cooler, Greene said, "What d'ya think, manslaughter one or two?"

"Two," his partner replied, without hesitation. "She'll walk in three years, tops."

Greene laughed. "She gets an all-woman jury, she may walk entirely."

"Hey! She blew the poor bastard away!"

"Yeah, but anybody who's ever spent a rainy weekend cooped up in a rolling thermos bottle playing Hearts is gonna see her side of it."

"Hmph."

"By the way," Greene said, "Sister Matty called. Macky and Billboard turned up zilch on the Carpenter kid up on Backus Ave, like we figured. Y'know, I got a feeling that kid's gone for good, one way or the other. Know what I mean? Harold?"

But Hafner wasn't listening. His thoughts were still in the I-room, still on the look on Susan Muncy's face and the image of that big blue camper sitting out on the A-OK lot.

He cleared his throat and said, "Uh, so, Kel, this Verelli's you keep talking up, the food is good, huh?"

"Yeah. Great pasta, and the Northern Italian cuisine is excellent too." Greene arched an eyebrow. "You know, I was only kidding before, that crack about you owing me a lunch."

"Actually, I was thinking of calling Marie," Hafner said. "See if maybe she'd like to go out for dinner tonight."

# CHAPTER 18

Death was as common in Father Joe Costello's life as a passing storm. It was something that came in its own time, in its own way. Sometimes there were early warnings of its imminence; other times it raised up from nowhere, wreaked its devastation, and disappeared just as abruptly. He was not a weatherman; he could not predict storms or even always explain them. His job was to help the survivors sort through the rubble after the howling winds died down, to lend them his strength, so that they might move on with their lives, at least until the next storm.

How many times in twenty years had he sat with a bereaved family, counseling them in their grief, murmuring prayers and soft words of assurance and hope and faith? He had held the hands of old people and AIDS sufferers, heard their last prayers and last breaths. He had been called to the scenes of horrific accidents, administering last rites upon the dying and the already dead. And, hardest of the hard, he had knelt before hospital beds in the children's ward of St. Mary's to bestow final blessings on innocent young cancer patients.

None were more difficult for him, more challenging to his faith and his natural optimism, than this death. "A better place," he intoned. "You've left us for a better place, my son."

"Amen," said Father Mazewski.

Both men made the sign of the cross and rose from their knees and took chairs. They were in the abbot's office, joined by Sergeant Podesta, who had remained seated during the impromptu prayer, feeling awkward. Now he cleared his throat.

"It's apparent the boy died of head trauma, as you could both see," the sheriff's investigator said, "but we'll know for certain once the medical examiner's office reports. Probably struck from behind with a blunt instrument, as we say. Maybe one of the rocks that was used to weight down the body. But that wouldn't account for all the other abrasions."

Father Joe sighed audibly, but he didn't speak. Couldn't speak, not quite yet.

Upon discovering the body, the sergeant had summoned the abbot to make an identification. Father Joe accompanied him, dreading every step down the grotto path to the pond, sensing that his worse fear was about to be realized. The first sight of the ravaged corpse sent a convulsion through him and he nearly lost what little he'd eaten that day. Despite the devastation and decay, there was no doubt it was the body of Sean Carpenter. He was dressed in tennis shoes, jeans, and an old Corpus Christi Youth Center T-shirt under a lightweight jacket. Tied around his waist was a canvas laundry sack, commonly used by all the monks. Instead of soiled work clothes and habits, however, this one contained five small boulders.

"Brother Jerome's missing rocks," Podesta said to the abbot, as they watched the crime-scene team go over the body. He then explained to the dumbstruck Father Costello the puzzling statement of the ancient hermit monk: what Brother Jerome had noticed that fateful night in the woods and what he'd observed since. "Now," the sergeant said, "if I can only figure out who fits the role of the bear the old man thinks he saw—"

Father Joe's eyes came up then, red-rimmed and wet but fierce. "I think I can help you with that."

\* \* \*

It was a warm, muggy summer day, but it was cool inside the foot-thick stone and plaster walls of the abbot's office. It helped that the office faced toward the east, away from the high sun of midafternoon.

Podesta's right foot nervously wiggled as he talked.

"When we concluded the body had to have been moved, I knew Sean couldn't have done that himself, so I started thinking about an accomplice. The name I came up with was Brother Chan—" The abbot began a protest, but Podesta warded it off with a wave. "—I know, I know, Father. None of your people were capable of such a thing. But forgive me if I can't accept that at face value. And it seemed to me that Chan was the best bet, being so dead set against expanding the bakery operation."

Father Mazewski wouldn't be silenced this time. "It was ridiculous before, Sergeant, and it's ridiculous now. Brother Chan would never harm anyone, let alone perpetrate two murders."

"You can relax. I've crossed him off my list anyway. He wasn't strong enough to move the body, either."

He told them about the medical examiner's latest finding, that it was probable Brother John's body had been moved by one person, carrying the dead weight over one shoulder. It would take a person of above-average strength to hoist and haul that much weight unassisted. That's why Podesta had asked that Chan be sent down to the pond earlier. He wanted to test the monk's strength by having him try to pull Podesta up from the muck.

"It was obvious that there's no way Chan could've carried Brother John's body."

"Carry it from where, Sergeant?" Father Joe asked, watching him intently. "Have you figured out where he was killed?"

"We think it happened in the bakery, just outside the office. Forensics found a tiny trace of dried blood on the steps leading up to the office landing. We haven't gotten the type back from the lab yet, but I'm assuming it was Brother John's. He and the perp apparently struggled there in the bakery."

"Or in the office," Father Joe said, "spilling out onto the landing and the stairs."

"Quite possibly," Podesta returned the priest's stare. "You wanna tell me why you think the office was the place?"

Father Joe steepled his fingers below his bearded chin and took a moment to marshall his thoughts. And to control his emotions. When he spoke, his voice was low but steady. "It seemed to me that this whole thing had to have something to do with the computer in the bakery office. That was the thing that had brought Sean here, made him useful to Brother John and the abbey. It was at the heart of the dispute between Sean and John— Sean's illicit use of the Internet connection to call up pornographic material."

"And Satanic materials too," the abbot interjected. "I don't know if you knew this, Joe, but Walter Monday said Brother John caught Sean accessing Satanic Web sites."

"Yes, Mr. Monday told me about that. He also said John discovered the problem by checking an electronic log kept by the Internet provider. At the time, I merely filed away the comment without examining it, but it nagged at me. Sean wasn't stupid. If there was such a log, why wouldn't he know about it and take steps to cover his tracks? And why *would* Brother John know about it? After all, he was the computer illiterate, not Sean. As it turns out, it's academic, since there is no secret log kept by the Internet provider. My young friend Mike Keller demonstrated that to me a short while ago." He paused. "There's no reason to think Sean ever accessed any Satanic Web sites."

"Well, then, why would Walter—" Father Mazewski began, but broke off. "Oh! You're saying Walter Monday—?"

"Is a murderer," Father Joe finished for him. "A man plenty strong enough to carry Brother John's body to the grotto and large enough to be mistaken for a bear by poor old Brother Jerome. He undoubtedly saw Monday while he was putting Sean's body in the pond."

Sergeant Podesta leaned back in his chair as far as he could go, looking for a bit of comfort that grew more elusive as the day went on. He crossed his arms over his chest, wished for the fiftieth time in an hour that he could have a cigarette, and said, "I'm assuming you've got more to go on than that stuff about Satanic Internet junk, Father."

"I do." The parish priest reverted to form, standing and pacing, just as he often did on many Saturday afternoons while he prepared his Sunday homilies.

First, there was opportunity. If, as Father Joe had surmised, the murder of Brother John had some connection to the new computer, Walter Monday qualified as the number one suspect. He was the only one, other than Brother John and Sean, who used the machine on a regular basis and was familiar with its software. Then, there's motive. If John's death wasn't the result of a conflict between himself and Sean, then what was it about? Money, perhaps? And where did money come in at the abbey? Through the selling of bread, a business that was almost wholly handled by two men, Brother John and Walter Monday.

Podesta interrupted Father Joe's narrative. "Slow down a minute. That's quite a leap you've taken—several leaps, in fact—without any hard leads to back you up."

"I had a lead, Sergeant." He told Podesta what Mike Keller had said, about Sean having something on Brother John that he could use to "take him down a peg."

"So he claimed to have something on Brother John," Podesta said. "Not Walter Monday."

"Yes. Which is why I dismissed it at the time. I could no more believe Brother John was guilty of any misdeeds than I could accept the idea of Sean Carpenter as a killer. But later, as I began to suspect Monday, it occurred to me that Sean may've found some discrepancies in the bakery's financial records. Discrepancies which he assumed were John's doing. But what if it were actually Monday who was behind it?"

"'It' what?" the abbot asked, frustrated. He was having difficulty following, or believing, any of this. "Do you have any proof that anyone has done anything?"

"Yes. I do now, thanks to Mike and his wizardry. And thanks to what a couple of my parolees found out earlier today from a member of Sean's old gang."

He told them about the call he'd taken in the bakery office earlier: Billboard relating Marco Pilato's claim that Sean had found proof of a scam involving the bakery's financial records and that he hoped to earn a reward for blowing the whistle. This had merely confirmed what Father Joe had already suspected, which is why he was in the bakery office in the first place—to have the Keller boy run a search on the office PC. A search that had turned up a list of seventy-nine files that had been deleted.

"Specifically, Mike found twenty-three data files, all spreadsheets, that had been deleted recently. These were files that had been created over the past year by Brother John and Sean, transfers of information from the old bookkeeping files into the new electronic system. Well, we couldn't make heads or tails out of them, but then Mike, bless him, found a file for an app that Sean had no doubt used to—"

"Wait, wait, wait," Podesta said. "A what? An app? What the hell is that?" He knew better than to curse in such surroundings, but too bad. He needed a smoke so bad he could hardly see straight.

Father Joe, whose pacing had sped up along with his monologue, sat down and took a deep breath to calm himself. "Okay. Let me explain it if I can. One of the deleted files Mike called up was from the installation of a special application that he thinks Sean created himself. It was based on a utility program called Audit!, only Sean had customized it to suit his needs. You with me so far?"

"Go on."

"The purpose of this utility was to check the spreadsheet files—all those old bookkeeping records that had been input into the computer—to search for errors and anomalies. Check the math, basically, and make sure correct bookkeeping procedures were followed. What it uncovered is a number of discrepancies. I won't call them errors, because they appear to happen too often and too uniformly to be errors."

"For example?"

"A rounding 'error' that shows up each week on each individual shipment to the various Wager's supermarkets. Mike pointed it right out. All the shipments have a dollar value, right? That's how much the abbey is being paid per shipment, per store. Well, the statements show that this is always an amount rounded to the last dollar."

"What's wrong with that?" Podesta said. "I do the same thing on my taxes, round the figures off to the nearest dollar. Makes the math simpler—"

"I didn't say rounded to the *nearest* dollar, Sergeant. All the subtotals in the statements we reviewed were rounded *down*, to the previous dollar. Whether it was, say, fourteen dollars and forty-seven cents or fourteen dollars and ninety five cents, the total was rounded down to fourteen dollars. We found this over and over, every subtotal, every week."

"Still," the sergeant said, "how much can it be, a few cents here and there?"

"By our reckoning," Father Joe said, "it averaged about eighty-four dollars per week, which figures out to better than four thousand dollars a year. And there's more. The audit found a discrepancy in the way unsold bread was counted." He looked to the abbot. "Tell him about the agreement you have with Wager's about unsold loaves, Father."

"Well, after two days on the shelf, any unsold loaves of Thy Daily Bread are delivered to soup kitchens and meals programs and other charitable enterprises throughout the area. You know yourself, Joe. The food pantry and meals programs at Corpus Christi get free bread every week from us."

"Yes, delivered by a Wager's truck. It's greatly appreciated, by the way. But tell Sergeant Podesta how the deal works."

"Well, it's quite straightforward. Wager's subtracts the wholesale cost of each unsold loaf from what it pays us for the bread, rather than sell it at a discount as day-old bread. In return for our agreeing to this, Wager's delivers the unsold bread for free to the various food programs. It works out quite well for all parties."

Father Joe nodded grimly. "Particularly for Walter Monday, it appears. A comparison of the percentage of bread sold each week and the amounts claimed as unsold shows that he was padding the unsold figures by several hundred loaves. Again, the dollar amounts aren't a lot per week, in this case only about forty or fifty dollars. But add it up, and then add in any other little tricks the man's been playing with the accounting. The abbey bakery grosses some two and a half million dollars a year, Sergeant. Monday told me that himself. He's probably taking in eight, ten thousand dollars a year, maybe more, by stealing a little bit here, a little bit there."

"My word!" the abbot said. "I never suspected a thing!"

"No one did," Father Joe said. "Until Sean came along with his computer programming smarts and his inquisitive mind. When he found out someone had been systematically stealing money from the accounts, he assumed it was Brother John. Maybe he even brought it to Walter Monday's attention himself. However it played out, Monday murdered Sean and John, hiding Sean's body so that everyone would think the young juvenile delinquent from the city had killed his mentor."

Both priests looked at Podesta expectantly. He had been listening carefully to Father Joe's story. Now he sat forward in his chair, his square face impassive.

"It's a nice theory, Father, and my guess is it's probably correct. But you've got no hard evidence to back it up."

"No evidence!" the abbot protested.

"What about the deleted files?" Father Joe said. "What about opportunity? What about the lie we caught him in, claiming John had caught Sean accessing Satanic Web sites?"

"Are there any fingerprints on those deleted files, Father? Can you prove it was Monday that erased them? Can you prove that Brother John *didn't* tell Monday that Sean was accessing Satanic Web sites? All Monday has to do is deny everything. There's no *proof*."

"There's the money he's stolen, the doctored financial records," Father Joe insisted. "It proves he had something to hide—"

"Maybe it does, if his lawyer doesn't turn it around and claim it was Brother John doing the stealing all along," Podesta said. "And even if we can convince a jury the man's a thief, we've still only got Monday for embezzlement. We have to have hard evidence, otherwise—"

Father Joe said, "What if we caught him in the act? I mean, trying to destroy evidence? Would that help, Sergeant?"

"Couldn't hurt. You have something in mind, Father?"

"It depends. Can you keep the discovery of Sean's body a secret for a few more hours?"

Podesta thought about it. "I guess so. The crime scene's been sealed off. There haven't been any media out here—"

"Then, yes. I do have something in mind."

# CHAPTER
# 19

The Mass that accompanied vespers was usually a quiet event attended by the monks, the novitiates, and sometimes a few tourists. On this Saturday, however, a steady stream of people began turning up beginning around 5:30. Their cars quickly overflowed the visitors' parking lot and lined the long gravel driveway bumper to bumper.

Brother John had been well known in Lorret County. As business manager for the abbey's bakery, he, more than any of the monks except the abbot himself, had been active in the community. The turnout for his memorial Mass was a reflection of his regard by those who knew him as a business associate and as a friend.

The chapel at the Abbey of the Ganannoqua was large as chapels go, but barely sufficient on this day. Most of the monks and the novitiates had arrived early and were already seated in the first several rows of pews. Behind them, the closest pews were filled with somber men and women, all wearing their Sunday best. Father Mazewski, who was greeting people at the chapel's main double doors, had shaken hands with several local suppliers and their wives: Mr. Michaelson, the raisin man; Mr. Dorrance, cooking oils and flour; Mal Wendt, the technician who serviced the mixers, ovens, and slicing machines. Also attending were the mayor and the entire village council from Garfield. Teachers, librarians, firemen, and farmers. Everyone, it seemed, who'd ever had a connection with Brother John.

It was gratifying to see, of course, but the abbot couldn't help but look over shoulders, stare past people even as he shook their hands and greeted them. For, of all the associates and friends of Brother John's to attend the Mass, there was one in particular whom Father Mazewski was hoping to see. But so far, Walter Monday had not arrived.

"Thank you for coming," the abbot murmured, shaking still more hands. "Edwin, it's good to see you. Hello, Mrs. Cramer . . ."

And then he was suddenly there: Walter Monday, looming behind a couple from Victorville whose names the abbot couldn't quite call up. Father Mazewski risked a glance over to the main entrance of the abbey, where Father Costello had been waiting out of sight.

Ah, yes, he was already moving, coming up to join Monday in the line. As planned.

"Walter, thank you for coming. Or should I say for coming back." The abbot held his hand and his eyes briefly. "Your second trip up today, hmm?"

"Yes, well, no problem, Father," the big man mumbled. "Quite a turnout—"

"Evening, Mr. Monday," Father Joe said, appearing at Monday's right elbow.

"Evening, Father."

"Joe, I'm glad I caught you," the abbot said. "Did you get the answer you wanted from that computer expert of yours? About—what was it? Checking out the software on the PC in the bakery office?"

"Doing a diagnostic analysis of the hard drive, actually," Father Joe said on cue. "And yes, my guy in Riverton called and said it was do-able." He looked at Monday, keeping his voice as casual as he could. "Sergeant Podesta thinks I'm crazy, but I had this theory that maybe something in the computer's files might tell us something about what happened between Sean and Brother John. Maybe find out if Sean had downloaded any Satanic materials from the Internet sometime within twenty-four hours of the murder, something like that. We're assuming he would've erased anything incriminating before he ran off, but there are ways to recall deleted material. We're going to have my man down tomorrow to give it a try."

"I—didn't know they could do that," Monday said.

"No, we didn't either," the abbot said. "Which is why Joe thought to call his computer expert in the city. Anyway, we'll know tomorrow if it was worth the bother. Meanwhile, gentlemen, I have a service to prepare for. If you'll excuse me."

The abbot made his way toward the altar, leaving Father Joe and the hulking bread buyer together in the apse. They moved to one side to let others pass.

"Filling up," Father Joe said. "I suppose we should find seats."

"Yes, well, you go ahead, Father," Monday said. He tried a grin. "A fellow my size, I'm better off standing at the back, out of people's way."

*   *   *

The sound of the brothers singing a familiar Psalm floated on the heavy air. At 6:40 it was still light out, the summer sun barely tickling the tops of the maple trees along the western hills. But there was no one about to see Walter Monday; everyone's eyes were on Father Mazewski and the big granite altar in the chapel.

Monday was sweating. Sweating like a madman when he entered the bakery and made for the short set of stairs and the office. He still didn't know how, but *somehow* he had to disable the computer. Kill it, *kill the damn thing* so it could tell no more tales. He yanked his handkerchief from the inside of his charcoal gray suit coat and mopped his face.

He thought he'd already done that, of course, deleting all those files. But he should've known better. They always have their tricks, these whiz kids and their computers. Like Sean Carpenter, clever little bastard. Too clever, as it turned out. If only he'd never come here, never hacked through all those old, redundant financial records—

*Damn.* It was way too late for "if onlys." What he needed now was a cool head. Yes, a cool head—don't panic again, Walter. A cool head and a plan. *A plan, goddamn it!*

It was as he neared the stairs, almost tripping as usual over a power cord that snaked out from under one of the giant mixers, that he came up with an idea. Maybe he could—yes! He would *fry* the computer's innards, give it a charge of electricity that would zap all its circuits, fog the hard drive so badly it would be useless. And no one could tell it wasn't merely an electical spike, a surge in the power system, an unfortunate overload.

It should work. It *had* to work. All he needed was an extension cord. He'd seen one around someplace . . .

*Yes!*

There was an orange heavy-duty extension looped over a hook along the wall next to the maintenance closet. He snatched it down and hurried back to the stairs, nearly stumbling as he stepped onto the landing and made his way through the familiar doorway into the office.

There on the corner desk, looking so harmless, was his nemesis. That goddamn PC, like some clacking, whirring conscience, dragging him down.

Well, no more. He'd see to that once and for all.

He reached around behind the machine and pulled its power cord out of the power strip that doubled as a surge protector. He plugged the PC's cord into the orange extension and headed back out the door. Then he stopped and came back to the PC. Had to make sure the thing was switched on. There, all set to go.

He paused again to take out his handkerchief and wipe away the sweat from his brow. He was swimming inside the suit, but that couldn't be helped now. If anyone noticed later, they'd chalk it up to his size and the closeness of the chapel, all those people crowding in. That was what would make this work, after all, keep him safe. All those people, facing the altar. He wouldn't be missed, standing there in the back. Wouldn't be seen slipping back in again, either.

All right now. The ovens or the dishwasher? Both were powered by 220-volt lines, twice the power of a normal circuit. But the dishwasher was direct wired. So he'd use one of the ovens.

Dragging the extension cord along, he sidled between the wall and the last of the three huge bread ovens and looked for the receptacle. It was there on the back wall. He unplugged the odd three-pronged plug that led from the oven, then paused. The plug end of the extension cord wouldn't fit into the 220 receptacle; it was shaped wrong. *Damn!*

All right. There was only one screw holding the plastic case over the receptacle. Remove that and the terminal connections would be exposed. All he'd have to do was touch the plug end to the terminals and zap! But—would he get zapped too?

He decided there was no time to worry about that. If he didn't act now, if they got their hands on those computer files, he'd have a lot more than 220 volts to worry about.

He fished a small jackknife from the depths of his pocket and used the blade edge as a screwdriver, removing the screw. The dark plastic case popped off the receptacle easily, and there were the three terminals, each with a thick copper wire wound around it.

He swallowed, feeling a dry lump in his throat. He wiped his dripping brow with the sleeve of his coat. Before he could think about it anymore, he shoved the plug end of the extension cord into the receptacle, wedging it in between the contacts, and held it there for a good ten seconds. Then he pulled it away.

Nothing obvious had happened. The cord seemed to get warmer, and he thought he could feel a slight tingle run through his arm maybe, but that was all. But, hey, what had he expected? It was at the other end of the cord that the damage was being done, inside the PC. Now permanently fried.

Chortling, almost giddy with fear and adrenalin, he replaced the receptacle cover and the screw and plugged the oven back in. He squeezed back along the wall to the aisle and headed back toward the stairs and the office, rolling up the extension cord as he went. When he stepped into the office, he looked up and saw Sergeant Podesta sitting at the computer desk, facing him, and holding in his hand the other end of the extension cord. Unplugged.

Walter Monday screamed and fainted dead away.

*    *    *

"Son of a bitch hit the floor like a load of wet wash."
The sergeant colored slightly. "Uh, pardon my language."

"Nothing to pardon, under the circumstances," the
abbot said.

"I'll second that dispensation," said Father Joe. "Did he
talk to you? I mean, about what he did?"

"Talk! I couldn't get him to shut up. I was trying to
read him his rights while Trabold cuffed him and the son
of a—pup was blubbering, laying out the whole thing for
me." Podesta shook his head at the memory. "I haven't
seen anything like it this side of Perry Mason reruns on
the cable."

The three men were standing beside the stone arch
that graced the formal entry to the abbey. Out ahead of
them, in the fading light of evening, was a red-and-white
Lorret County Sheriff's Department cruiser parked at the
top of the driveway circle. They could just make out,
through the tinted glass windshield, the bulky shape of
Walter Monday in the backseat.

"He admitted to both killings?" Father Joe asked,
staring at the cruiser.

"Oh, yes. With lots of whining about being a victim of
circumstances and never intending to hurt anyone and all
that. It's amazing how the perps always find ways to see
themselves as the victims. I mean, it's like he thought the
murders were almost justified. It's the stealing he felt he
had to explain."

It had begun, Podesta said, about seven years ago when
Monday's wife was dying of cancer. His Wager's medical
coverage included some large co-pays and didn't cover
prescriptions at all. So in the fourteen months that it
took his wife to die, he accumulated a debt of several
thousand dollars in medical expenses. That was when he
decided to jigger the Thy Daily Bread accounts. Nothing

personal, Monday had told Podesta. It was just that the unique relationship between the abbey and Wager's, with himself as the middleman, made it possible to manipulate invoices in ways he wouldn't have been able to do with his other accounts.

"He'd actually thought it up years earlier but never acted on it," Podesta said. "Not until the bills piled up too high, and Wager's turned down his request for a substantial raise. I guess, like a lot of other thieves, he started to believe that someone *owed* it to him, so he was just going to take it."

Monday had developed half a dozen different ways to slice pieces of profit from the abbey's account and slip the money into his own pocket. Brother John had always trusted the figures supplied to him by Wager's, and besides, the bread business had grown far larger and, thus, more profitable than he'd ever imagined possible. John had no reason to suspect anything underhanded was happening.

But the new computerized system would change all that. At first, Monday thought it only meant he'd no longer be able to manipulate the account; that his days of skimming were over. But then, shockingly, he learned from Sean Carpenter that the new software would be used to reconfigure and store the old, hand-entered bakery records. The potential that this would expose him caused Monday to begin cultivating the boy, encouraging Sean to come to him first if any "glitches" turned up. It might save him some embarrassment with the higher-ups at Wager's, he told the boy, if he were able to clear up any problems "in-house."

"So, when the kid did find all these so-called accounting anomalies," Sergeant Podesta said, "he went to Monday with it. I take it Sean thought that, since it was Brother John's job to keep the books, he must be the guy who was ripping off the abbey. Like you said, Father, the kid was probably mad at Brother John anyway, because of the run-ins they'd had."

Father Joe nodded dully. He had to ask the next question even though he wasn't sure he wanted to know the answer. "What happened? How did he manage the murders?"

"Well, he says he set the kid up by asking him to come back to the abbey on Wednesday night after all the monks were in bed. They were supposedly going to go over the accounts together, make sure the kid had his facts straight. Monday waited for Sean to come up the river road on his bike and, when he was still half a mile from the abbey, Monday ran him down with his car. Killed him instantly, he says.

"He took the bike home later, dismantled it, and scattered the parts at the town dump. But that night at the scene, he decided to sink Sean's body in one of the ponds at the abbey. He knew the vegetarian monks never fished in the ponds, so he figured it would be a safe hiding place. Everyone would assume the boy had simply run off.

"He got the body into the pond and then went back up to the bakery office to erase all the incriminating files," Podesta went on. "Unfortunately, he lost track of the time. When Brother John showed up early for work, he had no good explanation for being there. He made a show of leaving, then got a bread knife from the bakery, sneaked back to the office, and killed Brother John. He says he moved the body to the grotto so no one would connect the death to the computer."

"Thankfully, you did, Joe," said the abbot. He looked out again at the figure huddled miserably inside the cruiser. "May God forgive him his terrible sins."

"God forgive him," Father Joe repeated, following the abbot's gaze. "But I don't think I ever will."